Dark Angel

Sherry Fortner

Etsi Publishing Group
Atlanta

Etsi Publishing Group
Atlanta, GA

For details write Manager of Sales,
3420 Millwater Crossing, Atlanta, GA 30019

First edition January, 2014

The characters and events portrayed in this book
are fictitious. Any similarity to real persons,
living or dead, is coincidental and not intended by
the author.

ISBN-9781494277741

Printed in the United States of America

Dark Angel is dedicated ...

to my family, Ray, Denise, Jon, Lindsay, and Ian for listening when I talked of my book for four long years.

to my daughter, Jennifer Harper, who actually lives in Dacula, for her help and design of the cover.

to my friend and the first person to read the entire manuscript, Beth Howard, for falling in love with my characters and book.

The name of the LORD is a strong tower: the
righteous runneth into it, and is safe.
Proverbs 18:10

PROLOGUE

THERE IS AN ANCIENT, MYSTICAL TEXT which was written by Enoch, the seventh patriarch from Adam and the great-grandfather of Noah. Enoch tells of the angels who fell to earth. He tells their names, what secrets of Heaven that they taught mankind, and of their offspring with human women, the Nephilim or the Anak. The Anak, or the race of the giants, were a particular bloodthirsty race. The *Book of Enoch* says that they angered the Archangels because they consumed all of man's goods, and then began to kill men and drink their blood.

The Archangels went before the Holy One of Heaven to ask that something be done about the Anak who were killing God's creation. God tells the Archangels that he will turn the hearts of the Anak against one another so that they will kill each other off. This is where my story begins with the last of the Anak. It begins with the one who is unlike the others of his race.

1. FIRST ENCOUNTER

I WAS ONLY EIGHTEEN WHEN MY WORLD irrevocably changed forever. That was when I discovered there was a world around us of which most people were not aware. That was then, now they know. It all began in that exanimate time which stretched endlessly between Winter Break and high-school graduation. The time when I became conscious that there were dark beings in this world which wanted to destroy me.

The ball I was dribbling thudded against the sleek, hardwood floor seeming to deepen my trancelike state. My heart seemed to slow down in order to join its rhythmical beat. My surroundings seemed to fade into blackness as a dreadful scene from my past slipped into my vision. My mother's blank stare swirled around in the darkness. Her glazed, fixed eyes stared at me unseeing as the drumming of the ball pounded, pounded, pounded. The sound bounced around in my head until my pulse mimicked the beat.

"Annie, are you ill?" Kate asked. Then without waiting for my answer, she chattered on. "You've been standing there dribbling that ball for five minutes looking at the goal but not shooting. What's up? Dirty daydreams?"

I stopped in mid-dribble grabbing the ball and clutching it to my chest. Kate's last remark jolted me back to the present—basketball practice. Coach Neely's whistle screeched over the thudding of the basketballs ending practice and my need to answer Kate. I sent a shrug of my shoulders in her general direction.

Coach Neely had been my basketball coach for four years, and I still had not decided whether I liked him or not. Tall, dark and not very handsome, Coach was slim with slightly hunched shoulders and a perpetual haggard look on his face caused by the black circles around his eyes that began under his eyebrows and washed down his face to his cheekbones. Even darker than the circles, his black eyes gave his face a haunted appearance. He was not the kind of person you could warm up to. He never smiled, not once made a joke, or even laughed at any jokes the girls on the team ever made. His face never changed. His eyes were dull and lifeless. In his mid-forties, he had never married, and in the four years that I played basketball for him, he never dated as far as any of us knew. He was a loner, and the high school rumor mill swears he teaches high school just to coach basketball.

"Coach, may Annie and I shoot from the foul line for a little longer? Pleaseee," Kate urged. "If you let us, we'll wear our shortest shorts to practice tomorrow," pleaded my totally insane best friend who winked at me behind Coach's back. I knew Kate, and I knew she said that to Coach just for shock value attempting to get him to break the impregnable mask that was his face.

Kate has been my best friend since first grade. Strangers often mistake us for sisters. She has the same straight long hair the color of the sun at midday and blue eyes as I do. She is just shorter and more voluptuous than I. Next to Kate, I am built more like a stick. Though we look similar, Kate has a drop-dead gorgeous cherub face. Kate swears that I have a celestial appearance too. She says my fine features give me an ethereal persona. I tell Kate she should ride the short bus because I am not the beauty she thinks I am. She just loves me as a sister, and that love distorts her vision and her wits. I often wish we were sisters. I was only been five years old when my mother died in a car accident, and my distraught father never remarried. Kate is cocky and inappropriate most of the time, but I love her fiercely. Now, she just stands there popping her gum obnoxiously with her basketball resting on her jutting right hip staring at Coach.

"Bite me, Kate," Coach replied giving her a look so intense that anyone but Kate would spontaneously combust.

"Not even . . . ," Kate paused for dramatic effect glancing in my direction to let me know what was coming out of her mouth was going for the jugular, "if I were a shark, flea, fire ant, vamp, or desperate, would I bite you," Kate shot back.

"Is that the best you can do, Kate? You're slipping. You forgot bedbugs, wild dogs, and going to detention hall tomorrow at lunch. We'll see how that bites," Coach Neely smirked and began to walk away. He half turned back glancing over his shoulder and spoke to me ignoring the smoking look Kate was flashing him. "Annie, I'll lock up, but you can get out through the side door. Just make sure you have everything when you leave because the door will lock behind you when you go." Coach looked back at Kate and emphasized the word "everything" and gave a little grunt of amusement at the deadly look on her face.

"He is such a pain in the . . . ," Kate began but stopped short, exhaled deeply her shoulder slumping, and turned to me. "Do you mind staying for a while Annie?"

"No, my free throws could use some work," I answered solemnly, still trying to shake off the morbid thoughts and oppressive feelings weighing me down. Not even the image of Kate and Coach sitting in detention hall glaring at one another during lunch tomorrow could lift my spirits. We both focused on our shooting. Kate and I took turns. She would shoot, and I would rebound for her. Then, I would shoot, and she would rebound.

"Are you going with Jonny to Lauren's party on Saturday?" Kate asked never taking her eyes from the basketball goal.

"I guess I will. I hadn't really given it much thought."

I knew she was hoping that I was going to the party but without my boyfriend, Jon. She really wasn't a fan. She thought him a little overbearing at times. Jon and I had been hanging out, dating would be an overstatement of our relationship, since the summer between my sophomore and junior year. He is the quarterback of the high school football team, and most girls would give up their cell phone to date him. I basically saw him as more of a friend than a boyfriend. Jon was just a hang out buddy. I didn't have to go parties, dances, and games alone as long as Jon was around. I didn't want a boyfriend. I had things I wanted to do, and I didn't need to get attached to anyone who might sway me from my future plans. Jon, however, definitely saw me as his girlfriend; therefore, no other boy ever dared to ask me out which most of the time was fine with me.

Jon was definitely handsome in a jock kind of way. Muscular, tall, with dark hair and eyes, self-confidence oozing from every pore of his body, he was every girl's dream. I liked him, but I didn't love him. I thought of him in a more brotherly way, not very romantic. I enjoyed being around him, but that seemed to be it. If I did not see him for weeks, it would not bother me at all. Maybe I was just not normal. Maybe he was not my type. If Jon was not my type, what kind of boy would be my type? Jon seemed to be every other girl's type. So, what was wrong with me?

Once again, my thoughts seem to drift. Was it that I was not interested in Jon or any other boy because I knew something else was out there? But who or what was out there? My totally random thoughts were beginning to make me feel as though briefly, for a moment, perhaps I was going mad. My destiny whispered to me, and so did that something else. I did not understand all the confused, jumbled thoughts that tumbled through my mind and my soul. My heart almost ached for something or someone. But for what or whom did it ache? I am the girl of the hottest guy in school. For whom, was I searching? The whole problem is that I'm not looking for anyone. I am perfectly satisfied with the relationship Jon and I have as good friends. But yet something unknown was out there waiting for me — whispering our terminus a quo to me. I could feel it. I yearned for something, but what that something was, I had no clue. I believed I was being irrational, and no one else besides Jon and college was in my future. The basketball hit the rim with a dull thud. Quickly, I decided I should quit daydreaming and concentrate on my shooting.

"Who are you going to the party with Kate?" I asked trying to be polite and at the same time trying to get my mind off my depressing thoughts. "Knowing Lauren, I am sure it will be a major event."

"I think Austin will be the lucky guy this Saturday," Kate giggled rolling her big blue eyes.

Kate dated someone different almost every weekend. She was the school flirt, but she was harmless. Although, I don't think she would admit it, Kate, too, had an aversion to getting serious with just one person. She was outrageous, and the guys loved her. When Kate walked in a room, it was like she was on a movie set: lights, action, Kate. She drew the male population to her like moths are drawn to their deaths by a flame.

"You're such a tease, Kate."

"I know, and it is so much fun," Kate laughed hysterically.

Time quickly passed, and we were both absorbed
in shooting. The next thing I knew the gym felt like
we were in a freezer, and it seemed as if the lights had
dimmed.

"Kate, is this gym suddenly freezing, or am I
delusional?"

"You're right. It's really cold—colder than I was
last Saturday with Jeremy." She stopped in mid-
dribble and looked at me wide-eyed. "What?" She
said in response to my shocked expression. "He had
stanky breath," she giggled.

Shaking my head and sighing, I looked at the
clock on the wall. It was after eight o'clock.

"This is just great, Kate," I drawled out
sarcastically. "It's eight o'clock, and I need to study
for a biology test tomorrow."

"Sorry, Annie, I guess we lost track of time. I can't
believe that I went right past dinner and didn't
notice."

I shivered. Whether I shivered from the cold or
from the eeriness of Kate forgetting food for a whole
three hours, I wasn't sure. I glanced at Kate, and she
had her head tilted as if listening for something.

"Let's get out of here," I whispered. Kate and I
walked toward the locker room bouncing the
basketballs as we walked. The hollow, dead thuds
they gave in the empty gym threatened to pull me
back into the darkness and the black horror of visions
that I had experienced earlier during practice.

"Has Jonny asked you to go steady?" Kate pried
as we walked toward the gym dressing rooms.

"No, I've warned him about that when we first
started dating. I told him if he started getting serious
our relationship was over. So far, he hasn't dared to

pop that question, but we have been going out for over a year. I can tell he wants to get more serious."

Kate stopped suddenly looking down a dark hallway that entered the corridor to the gym. She continued to dribble the ball in place as she listened to me. Then leaning forward, she peered into the blackness of the hall.

"Annie, I saw a huge, dark something move in the shadows just now," Kate whispered.

I looked into the darkness. I took a step forward into the dark hallway. Even though I couldn't see anything, I could feel something. Something evil glared back at us, or at least that was the feeling I had. I glanced at Kate, and her face was ashen. I looked back into the dark void, and Kate grabbed my arm. I squealed and jumped in fright from her unexpected touch. The basketball I had been dribbling hit the toe of my shoe and bounced into the dark hallway where the blackness swallowed it up.

"Don't go after it, Annie. I have a bad feeling about this," Kate whispered grabbing my arm and pulling me back.

I hesitated, moving my head side to side peering into the darkness.

"I have to get that ball," I whispered to Kate, "Coach will kill us."

"It's not Coach killing us that I'm worried about," Kate whispered back hanging doggedly on to my arm.

"Why are we whispering?" I said aloud. My voice cracked and echoed back at me sounding weak and broken. "Wait here. I'm going to get that ball." Even as I said that, the ball rolled slowly back into the light stopping at my feet. Kate squealed a high pitch sound right in my ear.

"Who did that?" Kate yelled.

"It probably just hit a wall and rolled back to us," I told Kate in a trembling voice. I said it, yet I didn't believe my words. Someone rolled that ball directly back to me. It stopped right at the end of my sneakers. Stepping back, I scooped up the basketball and pulled her into the light of the locker room.

"It's probably just the night janitor, but I've seen too many gory movies about silly girls in an empty school building being stalked by a killer not to be a little uneasy. Let's just get our stuff and go." Kate must have been just as uneasy as I was because for once she didn't comment, but she hurried to the other end of the locker room in silence and began to gather her clothes which were strewn all over the bench.

I stuffed the basketball in the carrier that Coach left in the locker room. Kate tossed me hers and turned back to continue stuffing her clothes in her gym bag. I put her ball in the carrier then crossed to the bench and scooped my clothes and sandals from the bench and crammed them in my bag with my biology book. We didn't even bother to change back into our street shoes. Together, we hurried out of the locker room and crossed the gym floor.

"Was it this cold in here earlier?"

"Not even close," Kate answered shivering. The gym had cooled down some since practice, but it was positively frigid now. We were both shaking uncontrollably, but whether our shaking was from the temperature or from fright, I wasn't sure.

"Wait a minute, Kate." I murmured and moved to the double set of glass doors that were chained together and secured with a lock. I scoured the parking lot for anyone lurking around our cars. Kate's car was in a pool of light from the streetlight next to her vehicle, but still it looked eerie, surreal even. "It looks ok out there. Let's go."

We crossed the lobby to the side door.

"Get out your keys," I instructed Kate while I dug around in my bag for mine.

"We'll walk to your car. It's the closest, and it's parked under a streetlight. My car is parked in the back overflow lot. You can drive me around to it."

"Sounds good," Kate whispered her blue eyes wide as she looked furtively out the door.

The view of the parking lot wasn't as good from the side door, but I surveyed the parking lot again before pushing open the door. The cold, fresh air collided with my face and bare legs as it pushed its way inside. The walk to Kate's older model Chevy Blazer was uneventful but still creepy. Kate stopped once halfway to the car cocking her head to the side listening again. Then, without a word, she began walking briskly toward her car.

"How did we let it get to be so late? My dad is probably dialing the police as we speak," I squeaked trying to fill the silence with chatter while throwing my dead cell phone back in my bag.

Kate pushed the button on her key chain unlocking the doors to her vehicle, and we both climbed in.

"I was running late this morning. The only parking was in the back lot."

"No problem," Kate replied and crammed the keys in her ignition. Her Blazer started without hesitation. She sat up straight in the driver's seat and slowly turned facing me. "Annie what happened back in the gym was so strange. Stranger than Coach even."

"Ah, we probably just watch too many horror movies," I growled.

"Yeah, but it's fun being scared when you're crawled up on the sofa at home with a big bowl of popcorn. It's not so much fun when you're in an empty school building alone." Kate laughed her voice trembling.

"You weren't alone Kate. I was with you," I giggled weakly. "Maybe it was Coach trying to get even." The uneasy, dark feeling had not left me either, and I scanned the bushes, the parking lot, and the ball fields that ran along the side of the parking lot for anything that moved.

"Coach couldn't get even if I gave him the instructions," Kate growled. Then with an exasperated sigh, she turned. Kate looked at me her big blue eyes glistening with tears. "He already got even. I'm in detention tomorrow . . . and at lunch," she whined. "My social life is going to suffer terribly. I needed to network at lunch and see if someone hotter than Austin will ask me out to Lauren's party."

"You're so shallow Kate," I giggled.

"Extremely," she chirped. "I'll see you tomorrow morning in biology." Kate's mood instantly became somber as she pulled up next to my car. "Be careful, Annie," she warned.

I, too, had an older model SUV, a Tahoe, with only a small dent in the front right fender compliments of someone at a party last summer. It was the closest thing to a tank that my dad could afford. It still made him nervous for me to drive. If it was in his power, I would have a military escort every time I drove. If he was wealthy, I am sure I would drive a Hummer rather than a Tahoe. I pulled my keys out of my gym bag putting the panic button right under my thumb. I crawled out of the passenger side.

"Kate, make sure to lock this door back."

"K, I will. See ya Annie." With that, Kate just drove off leaving me in a cloud of dust in the darkness of the unpaved back parking lot.

I groaned. This parking lot ran alongside the baseball field and was not lighted. It was an overflow lot for the additional parking needed for home games and students, like me, who were so late for school that all the spaces were taken in the paved lots. I'll definitely have something to harass Kate about for the next few days. What was she thinking driving off leaving her best friend in the dark in a deserted parking lot?

As I turned toward my car, the uneasiness returned and began to seep into my bones. I felt the hair on my neck stand up. I pushed the button on my key to unlock my doors. Accidentally, I pushed the panic button instead in my haste to get the door open. The horn started blasting, and I jumped in fright dropping my keys on the dark gravel. I was still shaking, and I could not see my keys. I squatted down and swept my right hand back and forth trying to feel my keys.

A deep, throaty growl came from the darkness in front of my vehicle. My hand stopped, and my head lifted. Frozen, I remained still trying to figure out if I had indeed heard a low, threatening growl amid the blasts from my horn. I pushed my hair back from my face, and then I heard it again. It sounded only 15 or 20 feet in front of me. Even though it was a balmy, spring evening in Dacula, Georgia, a sprawling upscale suburb about twenty miles east of Atlanta, I shivered uncontrollably. I could hear the pounding thump of my heart accelerating, echoing in my ears. My throat tightened and constricted, so screaming didn't seem like an option. I doubted there was anyone around close enough to hear if I did get a scream out.

I could hear something moving in the darkness scraping and dragging along emitting a deep, rumbling growl that made my knees weak. I didn't know whether to stand up and see what it was or keep looking for my keys. I decided that I had to have my keys. I needed the protection of my car and to stop the blasting horn set off by the panic button. I was too vulnerable in the open lot. Dropping from a squat to my knees, I felt all around for my keys. I could hear the growling grow even deeper and coming closer. Finally, my hands hit the keys, but they made a loud scraping sound against the gravel in the parking lot. I panicked. Did that thing hear the noise of the keys? The growling and movement stopped for a moment. I knew then, that it did. I closed my fingers slowly, carefully around my keys and pushed the panic button again to stop the horn. I took that moment to collect my thoughts. What do I need to do? Racking my brain for a plan, I decided to push the button to unlock my doors, jump up while I pushing the button, yank open the door, and throw myself inside. Hopefully, I would surprise whatever was out there, and it would not react fast enough to get to me.

"At the count of three, Annie." Almost silently, I counted. "One . . . two . . . three."

I hit the unlock button and jumped up. However, instead of yanking the door open when I saw what was making the growling noise, I gasped and stumbled backward. I drew my fist up toward my mouth stifling the scream that was growing within me. Tears sprang to my eyes.

In front of me was a huge animal. It was as big as a small vehicle. The creature crouched yet stood on its hind legs upright. Its elongated, hairy, muscular arms were curled, yet at such a great length that they rested on the ground. The claws were broken and torn. Each thick nail curved crookedly for at least six to seven inches. Its mouth was open exposing several rows of teeth like a shark. Four to five inch jagged, pointed, yellowed teeth dripping with salvia crowded the creature's mouth, so that it gave the appearance of a demonic smile. The middle of its eyes was red encircled by a wide yellow band, and its eyes were fixated on me. The deep growl that emanated from its throat was horrific. It felt as though the ground under my feet trembled from sound of it. I had never seen anything so menacing. Its thick, shaggy, hairy coat looked black, though it was hard to tell as it blended in with the darkness of the night. Pulling its lips even farther back exposing more of its deadly teeth, it snarled. Salvia poured from its mouth in a stringy stream. I was about to die. This was it—the end. All I could think of was my father. If I am torn apart by a vicious animal and he loses me, it would surely put him over the edge. Tears ran from the corners of my eyes.

"Daddy," I whispered closing my eyes tight. I wanted my last thoughts in this life to be of my father.

The animal moved stealthily around the front of the car into a leaping position. It moved its body to face me head on, so the vehicle was no longer between us.

"Get in the car," I told myself, but I was frozen in fear, unable to move. I tried to make my limbs move, but it was as if they weren't getting the message from my brain. They felt as if they were bloated and weighed ten times their actual weight. Since the creature was less than fifteen feet in front of me, I didn't see how I could accomplish getting in my car before the animal got to me, but it was my only chance.

"Please," I whispered, "my Dad will die if I die."

Since my mother's death, I've had a crisis of faith, yet standing here faced with certain death, I pled to any unseen entity that might be in hearing distance to spare me. Then, if the situation wasn't desperate enough, something moved in back of me. I was still paralyzed with fear. Was there another creature? I strained to hear any further sounds coming from behind me, but my head stubbornly would not turn to look at what lurked there.

"Need some help?" a silky, deep voice materialized from the darkness. As if a switch was released, my limbs became my own again. I turned, seeing a creature behind me that was as frightening as the one before me. My mouth dropped open. I'm sure I looked deranged as I gazed at the sight standing behind me. Hovering above me in the darkness, his face shining with an alabaster glow, was an immense creature. He was gigantic, and he was absolutely, frighteningly beautiful. His large hand pushed me gently backward.

"Stay behind me." He ordered in a lovely, soothing voice.

This was unbelievable. This creature, I'm not sure I could call him a man, that stood between me and the

animal was incredible. He towered over me. His long
hair was the color of corn silk, and his shoulders were
broad and muscular. He wore no shirt, only a tunic-
like garment covered him from waist to knee. There
was a wide silver girdle that bound his waist. Silver
pieces of cloth that looked metallic hung at varying
lengths from the waistband. Huge muscular legs
peeked through the garment. He wore shoes like I
had never seen before. They were more moccasin-like
than shoes. They resembled boots in the respect that
they covered his calves; however, not like boots in
that they seemed soft and pliable. They were studded
in silver, and fine silver strands fell gracefully from
the studs. The tops ended right below the knee. Silver
rose from the top of his shoes covering his knees and
crawling up his muscled leg to leaf like points several
inches above his knees. The rest of him was bare, and
his garment swayed around him as though alive.
Three beautiful, delicately carved, silver sheaths hung
around his chest and back. The carvings looked to be
in some sort of language, but the only one I had a
good look at was the one hanging between his
massive shoulder blades. Two of them crisscrossed in
the front, and the third one, the one I could see the
best, hung from his back. I could not see his face as I
stood behind him, but I remembered it as lovely. His
size was definitely impressive too. For the first time
in long minutes, I felt as though I may live through
the night.

He crossed his arms, grabbed the hilt of a sword
in each hand and drew them slowly out. They made a
metallic swooshing sound as they parted from the
sheaths. The broad swords looked to be of the same
silver that the sheaths were fashioned from and
gleamed menacingly in the moonlight. The great

monster's crimson eyes narrowed at the sound, and he crouched lower in response. At that moment, the giant animal leaped for us. This massive angel who had come to my rescue dodged the animal slashing its chest and back as it missed us but not the point of his swords.

"Swords," I mumbled. "Where is a bazooka when you need it?"

This being that stood between me and the horrific beast tensed, but he did not speak. I moved with my gigantic savior being careful to stay behind him, but I watched the creature from under his outstretched arms. This being which stood between me and the monster was so incredibly large that I could stand under his arms and still have a foot of clearance. Light emanated from his skin giving it a stone-like appearance. I almost forgot the creature that was about to eat me, as I gazed at the one in front of me.

The animal screamed the most evil, hideous scream I could ever imagine and turned attacking again. The scream reverberated in my head until I realized that I was screaming too. The monster jumped for us again. This time my hero did not side-step the attack but took it head-on kneeling on one knee. I hung onto to his silver waistband like it was a lifeline kneeling behind him. He thrust both swords up to their hilts into the soft underbelly of the creature. The monster screeched hideously again and fell to the ground narrowly missing us. The creature twisted and tried to snatch the hilts of the swords with its massive mouth. My defender grabbed the hilts and jerked upward laying open the beast's belly which spat intestines squirming as if alive on to the ground. The creature lay at his feet snarling and growling sending streams of yellowed, bloody salvia pooling around its massive head.

My beautiful savior stood and pulled me up with him. He put his foot on the huge creature's side, and once again grabbed the hilts of his swords. The creature's head snapped around as its powerful jaws attempted to capture him between them. Deftly, he sidestepped its jaws. Then, he pulled his swords from the creature's body. They gave a great sucking sound as they slid from enormous wounds. Bloods spurted in deep, ruby fountains from them. He wiped the blood from his swords on the long fur of the creature and returned the two swords to their sheaths. Then, he reached behind him and pulled out the third sword. This sword was not metallic, and as he withdrew it, a flame flickered to life instead of a blade. It was unlike anything I had ever seen. It reminded me of a verse that my father read to me as a child. I'm sure he said that the Garden of Eden was guarded by a flaming sword. Being a PK, preacher's kid, I had heard the story many times, but I never took it literally or seriously. I still didn't. I had turned away from my faith after my mother's death. My dad went in the extreme opposite direction leaving his research position at a mega pharmaceutical corporation for the ministry. I think he wants to believe that he will see my mother again. That belief is what keeps him going and keeps him sane, but I know she is gone.

I was dazed. I was trying to wrap my mind around the events of the last few minutes. This could not be happening. Animals did not grow this big or strange. I have never seen an animal such as the one that lay before me now. It was the size of an elephant but looked to be a cross between a grizzly and a giant wolf with the deadly mouth of a shark. Killing an animal of this size with only a sword or two swords to be exact, I thought should be impossible. Even so, it had happened and happened before my very eyes. The light from the flame of his sword allowed me to get a better view of the monster. On closer inspection of the hideous creature, I gasped and shrank back behind my rescuer's enormous body. That animal was the scariest thing that I had ever seen.

This young giant used the flaming sword to separate the creature's head from the rest of its body. The monster's great mouth moved in response trying one last time to cause considerable damage, and then its eyes fixed into a stony glare. The strange being held the gigantic head by the shaggy hair on its top, and with his free hand, he flipped the flaming sword end over end. He caught it by the hilt as it came down and thrust the blazing sword into the heart of the great beast. The flame spread quickly across the creature's body cremating it where it lay. I was in a nightmare. I was sure of it. The flaming sword, the monster, this giant being, which came to my defense out of nowhere—it was surreal. I just wished I would wake-up; however, like Kate, I was shallow enough to want a better look at the creature left standing who had saved my life before I woke up. He was so incredibly hot, in a gargantuan sort of way, that I could only stare at him with my mouth hanging open. I must look like a lunatic to him. He turned and walked back to me carrying the head in one hand and returned the flaming sword to its sheath lying against his back with the other.

"Who are you?" I managed to get the words out even though I was hyperventilating.

"I am Zazel, son of The Watcher, Azâzêl. I am the last of the Anak."

"The Watchers? Who are the Watchers?"

"They are the Fallen Ones."

"Who are the Fallen Ones?"

"They are the hosts that were cast down from the presence of God."

"And the Anak?"

"I am they. I am the last."

"What was that?" I asked motioning toward the burning corpse.

"One of the Dark Ones."

"What is a Dark One?" I yelled out my voice becoming a screech in the eerie darkness.

"They are the Fallen Ones. They go by many names: Fallen Angels, Watchers, Grigori, demons, devils, and dark angels. Should I go on?" This magnificent creature waited for an answer as he loomed before me casually holding the dripping, bloody head of the creature.

I shook uncontrollably, but I managed to grind out between chattering teeth, "And who are the Watchers? This Grigori?"

"My father Azâzêl was one. Lucifer was their leader."

"I don't understand. Monsters are not real. The Dark Ones are not real. Fallen Angels can't be real," I reasoned since I didn't believe in them. "Leprechauns and little gray aliens are not real, and you are certainly cannot be real. Somebody wake me up!" I shouted into the black night. Even as I screeched this denial out, the evidence of the Dark One lay in a charred bloody mess at my feet.

I reached out to touch Zazel curious if he was really flesh and blood or another of my twisted dreams. As I touched him, he began to shrink slowly. I would guess he was over nine feet tall as he fought the monster. But now, slowly, but surely, he became a more normal size. He appeared more human, and he was easier to talk to now that he was more of a normal height. However, he must have still been six and a half feet or more.

"But I am very real, Annie." With that, Zazel took my trembling hand and placed in upon his chest. I could feel his heart pounding underneath my fingertips. Gently, I explored his massive chest with my fingers trying to determine if he was tangible—flesh and blood.

"You were scared too, huh?" I grunted nervously.

"No, not of the Dark One, He did not scare me for a second. You are the only creature that frightens me."

"Me?" I asked incredulously cocking my eyebrows to their fullest height. "You just killed a demon from hell, but I frighten you?" I used one hand to point at the creature and the other to point to myself puzzled.

"Yes," he answered solemnly and looked deep into my eyes. "I am accustomed to dealing with the Dark Ones. You, on the other hand, are something entirely different." He shrugged his shoulders and ran his fingers through my hair slowly letting it slip strand by strand through his fingers. He watched it fall as if in a trance. He raised a lock of hair to his nostrils and inhaled. Then he pressed it to his lovely mouth where he gently kissed the lock of hair. A warm knot began to form in my belly.

I was speechless. For the first time, I could clearly see his face in the glow of the burning carcass. He was

absolutely stunning. His was the face of an angel.
Every feature was perfect. His hair fell to his
shoulders, but on either side of his face, the hair was
braided in small braids. The braids were interspersed
with a silver chain that had silver stars woven into the
chain. Some of the stars were engraved in the same
strange language that I saw etched on his sword
sheaths. His jaw line was square and smooth, and he
had the most beautiful full lips. I had never seen lips
like that on a man before. His seemingly chiseled nose
was straight. There was something there in his eyes.
Some strong emotion cried out from them, but I was
helpless to know what it was. His beautiful eyes were
framed by long dark lashes. There wasn't really
enough light for me to tell what color they were, but
they were mesmerizing. They were burning a hole in
my face . . . and my soul.

"Who are you, and how do you know my name?"
I whispered again.

"I am yours," he answered quietly moving his
incredible body and breathtakingly handsome face
within centimeters of mine. Tenderly pushing a
strand of hair back from my face, he continued, "and I
have always known you Annie."

"Would you stop that? I don't know you. I have
never even seen you before. You are definitely not
mine, and how did you do that shrinking act just
now," I questioned him my voice rising in a panicked
screech once again.

He put his arm around my waist and pulled me
to his chest. My heart felt as though it stopped. He
crushed me to him lifting me off my feet. He held me
close with one arm for what seemed an eternity
staring down into my eyes. I could feel his body
shaking as if from fright or perhaps from longing. He

lowered his head and gently, very softly pressed his lips to mine. Instantly, I began to shake and shake violently. He was like a human Taser.

"Shhh," he whispered against my hair bringing up his other arm and folding me in an embrace. He held me tenderly until the violent shaking stopped. Nevertheless, I was in an utter state of confusion. I could not put a sentence together. The shaking changed to trembling. I could not remember my name or his. What was the matter with me? My thoughts were jumbled, and each thought pulled me in such a different direction that I could not think. I was paralyzed. I could see and hear, but I could not talk or move. The tears started to flow.

"Help me," I pleaded with my eyes. His eyes were locked on mine. He swept me off my feet never letting his gaze leave my face.

Gently, he placed me in the passenger side of my car and pried the key that I was still clutching from my fingers. Zazel walked around to the driver's side tossing the head of the creature up on the luggage rack. He climbed gracefully inside the vehicle and put the keys in the ignition. My lips would not move to ask him the question that I was trying to form in my head, but he seemed to read my mind.

"Please don't be frightened. The shaking and confusion when I kiss you is normal. You are human and I . . . I am not. Even so, Annie, you're safe. I am with you. We are together now, and that is all that matters."

Turning in the seat to face me, he leaned close his breath hot on my face. "I'm going to say this to you even though you won't remember it by daybreak. You are my heart, Annie. You are my one thought, my one desire, and my one need. All my heart has ever wanted for thousands of years is to be close to you. You are the knot in my heart that I have waited for millenniums to be untied. Yet, I fear we will forever remain like this. You, unaware of me, and I, hopelessly in love with you. Despite my feelings for you, I want you to forget what just happened to you. Forget me, Annie," he whispered gently as if his heart were breaking.

"All that matters?" I wanted to scream. "You just told me that you are not human." I wanted to rant and rave at him, yet I was moved by his passionate words. I wanted to pummel his handsome chest with my fists, but my brain was like gelatin. I could not open my mouth, but a single tear escaped from the corner of my eye. Gently, he caught the tear between his index finger and thumb. He stared at the tear captured there for several seconds. Then, never taking his eyes from my face, he ran his fingers slowly and lightly over my chin, traced the outline of my lips, my eyebrows, and down my nose back to my lips. He took my face within his long, elegant fingers and lifted my face to his.

"I have waited an eternity to speak to you, to hold you, Annie, but I need to get you home before I have to fight off the entire Dacula Police Force. Your dad must be worried. He will surely call the police if I don't get you home quickly." With that, he jammed the keys in the ignition and started the car. I could not speak. I could not move. All I could do on the ride home was gaze at him. His lovely words caused even more confusion as I was beginning to forget them, and I didn't want to. I wanted to hold them in my heart. He turned once and gave me a wide gleaming smile that caused my heart to flip flop within my chest. He acted as though he could hear the loud thumping of my heart and laughed softly. My head was clearing a little, though I still could not speak. If he could hear my thoughts, and what I would do to him if I was not paralyzed from his intoxicating kiss, he would not be smiling right now.

We turned into my drive, and he turned off the motor.

"Listen Annie, go straight in the house and upstairs to bed. You have had a most traumatic experience, and you need to rest."

Yes, I have had a most traumatic experience. Set upon by a creature from the very pit of Hell, and then saved by another inhuman creature that had the audacity to kiss me and whisper words of eternal love. Had he drugged me? No, the only thing he had done was very gently kiss me, but that is when all this confusion started when he first kissed me. Had he not said though that the effects of his kiss were because he was not human like me? Not human like me . . . I leaned my head back and closed my eyes in an attempt to stop my head from swimming. He came around and opened the door for me. He gently lifted me from my vehicle, and when I landed, I was standing beside the front door, gym bag in hand, and keys in the door. He unlocked the door and placed my keys back in my hand softly rolling my fingers one by one over them. He lightly captured my chin within his fingers.

"Good night my sweet." His lips were within centimeters of mine, and I could feel his warm, sweet-smelling breath. I closed my eyes and leaned toward him, yet he did not kiss me again. He just turned and walked down the steps sweeping the creature's head from the luggage rack as he strolled past my vehicle. He sauntered out into the night whistling a haunting melody and swinging the great beast's head by its hair.

2. NEW GUY

I AWOKE THE NEXT MORNING FEELING like I had a hangover. How is this possible? I hadn't drunk anything alcoholic. My head throbbed in response to that thought, and I felt nauseated. The sun streamed through my window. The sun? Briefly, I wondered what time it could be. I glanced at the clock, 9:05. I bolted straight up in the bed. It simply couldn't be. My biology test was at 8:00 a.m. I rolled from my bed, but my legs didn't catch me. I fell face-first into the floor. Groaning, I crawled to my knees pulling myself up with handfuls of my comforter until the upper half of my body was lying back on the bed again. Wobbling, I rose more carefully this time and stumbled to the bathroom. What was the matter with me? My body was simply not responding to normal functions. I turned on the shower hoping a hot shower would make me feel better.

Awkwardly, I tried to wrap a towel around my hair three times before it stayed well enough to shower. I certainly didn't have time to wash my hair.

I stepped into the shower. For minutes on end, I allowed the scalding water to soak my body. Then I scrubbed all over, shaved my legs, and turned the hot water to cold water. Shivering, the chilly water did the trick rousing me from my stupor instantly.

I jumped from the shower. There was no time for make-up and

hair styling this morning. I ran the brush through my long, tangled hair and pulled it back into a ponytail. I brushed my teeth so vigorously that I spit out blood when I rinsed the paste from my mouth. Pulling on a pair of jeans and a sapphire sweater, I slid my feet in a pair of blue, sparkly flip-flops on the chance it would be warm enough today for them. I reached for my purse, gathered my gym bag, and snatched books from their resting places as I went through the house. Inside my vehicle, I rummaged in my purse for a pair of sunglasses to protect my throbbing eyes from the sun. Backing out of the drive, I headed for school a good hour and a half late.

Since I was late for the second morning in a row, the only parking left was in the back lot again. As I pulled into the lot searching for a parking place, panic gripped my chest and squeezed. Something happened here. I could feel it, but I couldn't put my finger on the memory. Perhaps, it was just the dreadful nightmare that I had last night and not an actual event. I searched my brain for details. I felt

something happened here in the parking lot when I left the gym after basketball practice. Then someone or something helped me. The whole memory was fussy, but I didn't have time to dwell on it. I had a hike ahead of me to the school office. I opened my door and stepped out of my car right into a pile of ashes.

"Ew, disgusting!" I complained wondering who would have a bonfire in the parking lot. I stared at those ashes for long seconds. I looked around searching for something to jog my memory, but the only thing that seemed to want to tug at my memory was that piles of ashes. What could I possibly have to do with a pile of ashes in the school parking lot? Looking at my dirty, sooty feet, I felt like climbing back into my car and going home. I paused indecisively. I really needed to be at school. Final exams were in a few weeks.

Still grumbling, I ran the 300 hundred feet from the back parking lot to the school office. I opened the office door to sign in tardy breathing heavily. Some big oaf was half lying on the counter flirting with the office staff when I stepped inside the suddenly too small office. The object of every female's attention straightened up as I stood behind him trying to get to the sign-in book. My breath caught in my throat as he slowly turned around. His pearly white teeth gleamed in a dazzling smile against the backdrop of a perfectly chiseled, tanned face.

"Annie," murmured the strange young man who was handsomely dressed in a pair of designer jeans. He wore a white button-up shirt with one of those expensive logos on it. He looked like a male model, but he was much more handsome. Any model or actor whom I had ever seen would seem only mediocre in comparison.

"Do I know you?" I asked irritably.

"We have met," he winked at Mrs. Woods and spoke in flawless English; although, he sported somewhat of an accent that actually sounded middle-eastern. He flashed another gorgeous smile that seemed vaguely familiar.

I stared at him blankly.

"I was telling Mrs. Woods and Ms. Lindsey how we met in Europe last summer. What a coincidence that I have moved to this area."

"I don't recall . . . " I began.

"Annie!" It was Mrs. Woods' loud, obnoxious voice that roused me from the dreamlike state that I was falling into when this stranger spoke to me. "Sign in and show Mr. Starr the way to third period," she stated harshly.

Mouth open, I could only stare at him. Who was this person? I thought again that I might know him. Perhaps, I might have met him last summer like he said. Last summer, some young people from my dad's church and I hiked across Europe. It was incredible. That trip was the most amazing experience of my life, and I think I would remember meeting this guy. I was in a state of confusion again. I could not get the memories to come.

"Don't fret, Annie," he whispered. "Here, sign in," he said as he handed me a black pen. Mechanically, I did as he suggested.

"Ladies, it has truly been a pleasure to make your acquaintance," he gushed catching Mrs. Woods' hand in his own and pressing his lips to her fingers.

Mrs. Woods, the school secretary and meanest woman at Mill Creek High School, was putty in his hands. She giggled like a school girl for goodness sakes. I was embarrassed for her, but I could only squeak when I tried to voice my displeasure. He winked at Ms. Lindsey, the guidance counselor, and opened the office door for me. What is this guy's deal? If he hadn't been there, Mrs. Woods would have raked me over the coals for twenty minutes as to *why* I was late again for the second day in a row, and *did* my dad, the pastor, know that his daughter could not even make it to school on time.

"Shall we?" he asked. "Let's see. This is third period according to this schedule, and we need to be in English." I followed him into the hall like a puppy. He stopped beside my locker, flipped through the combination, opened my locker, threw my gym bag and book bag into it, pulled out my English book and notebook, and slammed the locker shut all with one hand. How did this person know my combination and the location of my locker? I was frightened. He had to be a stalker. There was no other explanation. He reached for my hand and led me through the halls like he was being guided by a navigation system. I was in a shocked state of silence. He said he was new. Then, how did he know his way around school like he did? The atmosphere was charged. It was like I was walking through a fog, but I was watching myself from afar. He was with me in the fog. This gorgeous, magnificent creature who was guiding me through toward the light.

Struggling, I shook my head to clear it and found my voice, "I need to stop by the restroom," I whispered as I lifted a sooty foot.

"Of course," he replied relinquishing my hand.

I leaned against the sink and drew in a deep breath. Raising my head, I looked at my pale reflection in the mirror. I looked like the same girl that I was yesterday, yet somehow I knew that I would never be that girl again. I turned on the water and let it run over my hands. Transfixed, I stood there for minutes on end just watching the water tumble over my palms and fingers.

"Annie, are you ok?"

I groaned inwardly. I had hoped he would go on to class without me.

"Just a minute." I pulled wads of paper towels out of the dispenser and wet them. Pulling my flip-flops off, I laid them in the sink letting the water rinse them off while I washed my feet. I slid them on after drying them with subsequent wads of paper towels, turned my back to the sink, and leaned against it. I took a deep breath. I wasn't sure what was going on, but I was determined to face it head on. Saucily, I slipped into the hall walking right past Zell.

I had not gone five steps before he was beside me and holding my hand once again. His presence made me want to weep, and a tear slid from my eye as we rounded the corner in the hall. Just like the tear that escaped from my eye, my determination slipped too. He stopped outside the door before going in the classroom. He noticed the tear falling from my cheek and crushed me to him.

"Oh Annie, don't cry, please," he begged.

I couldn't answer, but more tears spilled out of my eyes in response to his tenderness. Why was I crying? I had no reason to cry. Perhaps, it was just that I was feeling rotten this morning. I was late to school. My feet had gotten filthy and now him. I felt as if suddenly I knew the answer to the soul searching I had been doing, yet I wasn't sure what the answer was. It was as if my destiny was embodied in this young man, but I didn't know him or the destiny that he represented. I refused to believe my destiny was tied to any person of the opposite sex.

I was determined not let this guy get to me. I rebounded and recoiled from his touch.

"Get your hands off of me. I do not know you," I spit out. "You can tell Mrs. Woods and Ms. Lindsey any fantasy you like, but I know the truth. The truth is that I never met you in Europe. The truth is that I have no idea who you are. Tell me. Just who are you? How do you know my locker location and combination?"

"Forgive me, Annie. My name is Zell Starr," he said as he swept into a low bow introducing himself.

At the sound of his name, a ferocious beast leaped at me from my nightmares, and I shuddered and reached out leaning against the wall for support. I must be going insane. At a word or touch from him, I would have a vision from my many nightmares. It was as if scenes from my nightmares were cut and pasted into my morning.

"What kind of name is Zell? For goodness sake's stand up," I said exasperated.

He immediately cut his exaggerated bow short and stood up. I gazed up at him. He was absolutely stunning. His hair shone as if a halo enveloped his head. His long, light hair was pulled back at the nape of his neck with a silver band. His face was that of an angel. His teeth were perfect and amazingly white. He had a well-placed dimple below each of his cheekbones. He had the most unusual eyes that I had ever seen. His eyes were silver, perhaps some people would call them gray, but to me they were the color of rain clouds in a summer sky. His tanned skin set them off, intensifying the color. His smooth, Mediterranean skin was a stark contrast to his light eyes. I had never seen any human's eyes as beautiful as his. He was meticulously dressed, and he smelled heavenly.

"Zell?" I whispered more in a question than a statement.

"Yes, love," he grinned, and his smile was so dazzling that I felt my knees grow weak and buckle.

"Are you ill?" he asked.

I shook my head no without looking at him.

"To answer your question, Zell is an old family name. It dates back in my family thousands of years. Come, let's get this over with," he sighed. His right hand slid down my arm and gently folded around my fingers. Slowly, he opened the door to English class and pulled me inside the room with him.

He walked confidently across the room to where our English teacher, Rachel Edge, stood before the board.

"Good day, Mrs. Edge. I am a new student, Zell Starr, recently transplanted from a small country in Europe, Monaco." Zell held out his hand to Mrs. Edge. He continued to weave his magic on her and the rest of the class. "Annie was in the office as I was finishing up with registration, and she was good enough to escort me to class. Here is her tardy admit," Zell handed her my admit slip and his registration papers as he finished speaking.

"A pleasure to meet you Mr. Starr," Mrs. Edge replied somewhat puzzled as to why he was holding my hand.

"Hmmm," she nervously cleared her throat. "Since you and Annie have already been introduced, why don't you sit in the vacant seat next to hers?" She motioned toward two empty seats.

"Thank you, Madam."

Did he just say Madam? Who in the twenty-first century says madam? Who was this guy? If a girl from the Deep South thinks he talks old-fashioned, he's a Neanderthal. With that thought still tumbling through my head, Zell pulled me toward the two empty seats in the back of the room.

I couldn't bear to look at the shocked expression on the face of every student in class and kept my gaze fixed on Zell's back. The word "shocked" doesn't even do the looks on my classmates' faces justice. Mouths were literally hanging open. I fabricated a smile that I am sure looked more like a tortured grimace and followed him. Every head turned as we passed and watched as we were seated.

Mrs. Edge rapped hard on her desk trying to get everyone's attention. However, no one paid her any notice. Everyone, without exception, was still turned with their eyes on us. I could feel the girls in class melting at Zell's remarkable good looks, and I could feel little green monsters of envy eating away at the boys in class for the same reason. Mrs. Edge rapped repeatedly until the rubber head flew off the small wooden hammer she was abusing and hit Butterbean, alias Scott Brett, in the back of the head.

"Ow," Butterbean yelled rubbing the bump on his head. Scott had become affectionately known as Butterbean years ago in elementary school when he brought a plastic bowl full of the overblown beans to school for lunch. One of his friends aptly concluded that Scott resembled his lunch, pale and fluffy. From that moment on, Scott was called Butterbean by everyone under the age of 18 and occasionally by parents and teachers.

[35]

"Class, please! Please resume working on your essays," Mrs. Edge said loudly. "Sorry Scott," she added dryly as he retrieved the hard rubber hammer head from the floor and laid it on her desk.

Slowly, reluctantly, knowing there was a juicy story to be heard later behind our entrance, one by one, the class turned back around in their seats and resumed their essays.

Zell opened his notebook and began completing an essay about the assignment written on the board: Compare and contrast the characters in Hamlet. He wrote quickly in an elegant handwriting. I sat there like a lump of coal pen in hand staring at a blank sheet of paper. He tore that essay out of his notebook and began another. I watched in shocked silence as he headed the second one in my name and wrote it in my handwriting. How did he know what my handwriting looked like? He copied it to perfection. This was getting stranger by the second. I began to really be afraid of this guy. I admit I was a little relieved that he was taking on my assignment himself because I still sat there, pencil in hand, in a fog with a blank piece of paper in front of me.

"How did you know?" I managed to squeak out.

"I know everything about you Annie,"

"How can you just walk in here and write out an essay about the characters in Hamlet? Have you read it before?" I continued on in a whispering monotone tirade not waiting for an answer. "Wait, what do you mean you know everything about me? Are you a stalker?"

Zell laughed. "No, I only have your well-being in my heart. After I met you in Europe, I admit I was interested in you. I found out all I could about Miss Anna Hayes. To answer your question, however,

Shakespeare was a talented man. I have read all his work, and I even acted in a couple of his productions," Zell answered.

"You mean at school in Europe?" Annie asked.

"No, I mean at the Globe Theater," Zell retorted.

"What are you talking about? The Globe Theater burned in 1613."

Zell only smiled and winked.

This morning was getting out of control. "How can you write exactly like me?"

"It's quite easy. Chicken scratch is actually a breeze to imitate," Zell chuckled pleased with his little writing job and flashed another brilliant smile.

I groaned. Next to his elegant penmanship, which was a cross between Old English Calligraphy and modern cursive, my handwriting did look like chicken scratch.

"Just stay away from me. People are getting the wrong impression. Everyone is staring. My boyfriend will be furious. Besides you are creeping me out," I whispered none too delicately.

Zell looked at me and smiled, but I could detect sadness in his eyes. Immediately, I felt ashamed for saying he creeped me out. There were a lot of words I could use to describe him, but creepy was definitely not one of them. I turned my back to him and waited for class to end. I waited in dread for the bell to ring— to face all my friends who would be full of questions. I shouldn't have worried though because as soon as the bell rang, all the girls and a few of the guys crowded around to introduce themselves to Zell pushing me to the outside of the circle. I was forgotten. I saw the lovely LeeAnn latch on to Zell's arm and pull him toward the door. That was fine with me; let LeeAnn have the stalker. Turning on my heels, I huffed out of the door.

I hurried to lunch. I overslept and did not have time for breakfast. Today, I was thankful that seniors had early lunch because I didn't remember eating last night either. In fact, I didn't remember anything that happened the previous night after basketball practice. I did know that I was hungry now, and I moved to the hot lunch line. Today, my usual diet of salad at lunch wouldn't do. I wouldn't be able to eat it fast enough. I was ravenous, and I wanted something I could scarf down quick. I settled for a hamburger and fries. School hamburgers were rather lame, but I was in no shape to be a food critic today.

I was halfway through my hamburger when I saw the lovely LeeAnn enter the lunchroom with Zell. I was amazed once again at just how gorgeous this guy was. The word handsome didn't even do him justice. He was beautiful, dazzling. Movie stars would be jealous of him. Even if he were a moron, I bet he could go to Hollywood and get a contract for a million dollars just to let people look at him. What was a guy like that doing in Dacula, Georgia? A small knot of anxiety, maybe fear, began to grow in my belly. My half-eaten hamburger dangled from my hand suspended in mid-air while my mouth hung limply open watching Zell and LeeAnn. I tried not to watch him as he walked with her to the salad bar, but I could not tear my eyes from him. It was as if he was magnetic north, and I was magnetic south. Everything in me wanted to gravitate toward him. He turned his head and looked straight at me. His mysterious eyes locked with my eyes. I saw a smile, smirk was more like it, tug at the corner of those luscious lips. Rylee walked up and locked her arm through his on the opposite side from LeeAnn. She tilted her head up to speak to him, and he pulled his gaze from mine and bent his head and whispered something in her ear. She giggled so loudly that I could hear her from where I sat thirty feet away. I was so lost in thought that I didn't even notice when Jonny sat down beside me.

"What are you staring at?" Jon asked following my eyes to Zell, Rylee, and LeeAnn.

"There is a new guy at school who moved here from Europe. He is in my English class, and he says he met me last summer. I was just trying to place him. I don't remember him at all. I think if I met him that I would remember him. He is so . . . so unusual looking," I replied curling my nose in disgust.

Jon narrowed his eyes continuing to watch Zell, Rylee, and LeeAnn at the salad bar. "Looks like he's hooked up already."

I frowned. Somehow that comment bothered me, and I had no idea why it should. Reluctantly, and with every ounce of willpower I possessed, I drug my gaze from Zell to Jon. Out of the corner of my eye, I could see Zell and the two girls sit down at a table parallel to Jon's back. Zell's questioning eyes met mine and locked there. He stared at me while Rylee and LeeAnn chattered on and on. I was lost in his gaze.

"Annie . . . Annie did you hear me?" Jonny asked as he began to turn around to see what I was staring at now. I grabbed his arm to stop him from catching me watching Zell again.

"I'm sorry. What were you saying? I was lost in thought. I got up late this morning, and I missed my biology test. Kate's in detention hall with Coach, and I'm just not all here today," I said apologetically.

"I was saying are we on for Lauren's party this weekend?"

"Oh yeah, sure," I answered automatically with a hint of regret. Why did I feel this way? Why was I regretting making a date with my boyfriend? I didn't even understand me anymore.

"What did you say happened to Kate?" Jon asked looking around the lunchroom.

"Don't you listen to me? Kate is incarcerated in detention with Coach," I mumbled chewing on a fistful of fries. I was thankful when the bell rang to go to class and rescued me from anymore conversation with him.

"Humph! Poor Coach," Jon snidely remarked.

Jon walked me to Civics after carrying both our trays to the hole in the side wall of the cafeteria where an attendant slapped them against a trough and stacked the trays in a container for the dishwasher.

Stopping outside the door, he tried to kiss me, but I alertly dodged his mouth. "Miss Howard will write us up if she sees us kissing in the hallway," I hissed at him.

"Ah, Annie live dangerously for once," Jon groaned throwing his hands up.

"Not a chance. My dad is a minister. If I get written up for making out in the hall at school, he will freak. My life is impossibly dull, and that's the way I want it. I'll see you later," I said ducking under Jon's outstretched muscular arm that was propped once again against the wall attempting to prevent me from entering class.

When I entered the room, I was disconcerted to see that Zell had been watching our exchange intently. I was not sure I read the look in his eyes correctly, but he looked jealous. He looked deadly, and I was a bit unnerved by what I saw. I was also dismayed to see that Jon had kept me in the hall so long that the solitary open seat was next to Zell. If only Rylee and the lovely LeeAnn had been in Civics, I wouldn't have to worry about the seat next to Zell being available.

With a plop, I sat down and banged my books on the desk.

"Lover's spat?" he leaned over and asked.

"*If* . . . ," I said hesitating for effect and raising my eyebrows so high that I was sure they were lost in my hairline, "it's any of your business, no. Jonny can just be so . . . so clingy at times," I remarked irritated. "Are you in all my classes?" I asked even more irritated by that possibility.

Zell laid his schedule on my desk. "I think I may be. Here, check my schedule."

I recognized immediately that he was. He was in every single one of my classes. How did that happen?

"Yes, it appears that you are in all of them," I groaned slapping the schedule back on his desk. "How much did it cost you to be able to irritate me all day, each and every day?"

"Does it really bother you that I am in all your classes?" he asked perplexed.

"The only thing that bothers me is that I will have to spend an exorbitant amount of time avoiding getting drool all over my clothes from your female admirers," I gritted out.

Zell laughed out loud. It was a hearty, manly laugh that gets into your soul and immediately lifts your spirits. In spite of myself, I gave a half-hearted grin.

"Are you jealous?" he asked leaning close making sure Mrs. Howard's back was turned as she wrote on the board.

Horrified, I turned to face him with my mouth hanging open in disbelief.

"Jealous? Give me a break. Why would I be jealous? I have a boyfriend."

Zell laughed again softly this time and looked into my eyes not blinking. His silver stare paralyzed me. Thankfully, Mrs. Howard began to lecture, and with great effort, I broke contact with his eyes and moved mine to my book.

When the bell rang at the end of class, I was jolted from my trance as Zell took me by the elbow and lifted me up.

"May I walk with you to your next class since it is also mine?" he asked.

"What is with you and the manners? You talk like you're from another century." I pulled my elbow from his grasp and shrugged my shoulders in reluctant agreement. I didn't understand why I was being so rude to this guy. I really should cut him some slack, but I was actually beginning to enjoy the verbal banter.

He grinned obviously unaffected by my sarcasm.

"Tell me what is there to do in Dacula?" Zell asked as we walked down the hall.

"Basically not much, but we are only about thirty minutes outside of Atlanta. There is plenty to do there: museums, an aquarium, a zoo, professional baseball, football, and basketball teams, theater, concerts, parks."

"Hmmm, sounds like there will be a lot for us to explore together."

I snorted and turned to tell him it would be a cold day in . . . , but he was already handing his admit slip to a teacher that was substituting for Miss Picknell, our art teacher. She had taken a class of juniors to the High Museum in downtown Atlanta today, and a substitute was here in her place. I said a mental thank you when the sub slipped in a video about Leonardo Da Vinci. I knew I wouldn't have to look at or talk to Zell while the video played. He was a nice guy, but everything about him disconcerted me. The sub slipped the DVD in to play on our large-screen Smart Board. He flipped off the lights. The room went into total darkness. The art room had very high ceilings for some unknown reason, and there were no windows. It was so dark that anyone could do anything in this room with the lights off and not be seen. The only light emanated from the video on the screen. Sitting together at the last table in the art room, Zell was so close that I could smell his scent. It was intoxicating. I didn't know what kind of cologne or aftershave he wore, but it definitely worked. He leaned close, and where our bodies touched a flame seemed to burn on my skin. It was hard to think of anything but him. I folded my arms on the art table in front of me and lay my head down on them closing my eyes. I had nightmares last night and had not slept well. I was tired and becoming drowsy. Besides if I closed my eyes, maybe I would forget Zell was next to me.

He leaned even nearer in the darkness, and his hand enveloped mine in the dark. I jumped like I had been shocked. I lifted my head and turned it sharply. I bumped into his face, hard.

"Zell is that you?"

"Yes," he answered.

I breathed heavily, and I felt his lips travel a short distance as he sought my mouth. He kissed me gently. Just wait until I tell Jon, Zell would be dead. Even as the thought flickered through my mind, I knew I could not tell Jon. I didn't want Zell to stop, and that thought terrified me. He kissed me again passionately. I began to shake and slip from my seat, but he caught me and pulled me to him. I felt as though we moved in that embrace. I was sure now that we had because I felt the wall pressed behind me. Zell pressed against the front of me as I melted into a corner of the wall which was on either side of me. We must have been in a corner in the back of the room. My breath became ragged. I felt dizzy and unable to stand, but Zell held me. He kissed me softly and tenderly. I wound my hands against his neck and began to return his kiss. I pressed against him, and he held me in an embrace so desperate that I didn't know if he would ever let me go. I met and matched his passion. I knew I shouldn't, but I was unable to stop myself. It was as if all else had ceased to exist except the two of us. Quivering, I felt as though I would lose consciousness.

"I'm sorry Annie. I shouldn't kiss you like this, but I have waited so long for you that I can't help myself," Zell whispered his sweet breath hitting my face like a heater causing my own breath to catch in my throat. "Just being able to touch you after all this time . . . " his voice trailed off.

I awoke as bright fluorescent lights flooded the room. I lifted my head from my arms that lay folded across my books on the table.

"Have I been asleep?" I asked Zell.

"It appears that you have. As soon as the lights went off, you laid your head down," Zell answered.

"I had the strangest dream," I croaked.

"What was it about?" Zell asked cocking a finely shaped eyebrow.

"You, so it must have been a nightmare not a dream," I responded curtly, stretching. Even as I said it, I cringed. I scolded myself. I shouldn't encourage him by telling him that. I didn't know what was wrong with me. Now, my dreams and nightmares were invading my daytime too.

"Really? Why would you dream about me?" Zell replied looking at me strangely.

"I don't know. It was the strangest experience. I could swear it actually happened." I looked at Zell, and there on his face was what appeared to be pink lipstick. The color seemed to be the same as my hot pink shade of lipstick. There were two smudges. One was just above his lip and the other on his right cheek.

"What?" he asked as a response to my dumbfounded expression. I took my index finger and wiped the smudge of color from his face and lip.

"Where did this come from?" I asked him point blank waving my pink fingertip in his face. "It looks like my pink lipstick is on your face?"

Zell pulled a cherry Tootsie Roll Pop from his shirt pocket.

"I'm addicted to these," he said smiling and picked up his books popping the freshly unwrapped Tootsie Roll Pop in his mouth. "See you tomorrow

Annie," Zell whispered leaning close. Without looking back, he strode out the door with half the girls in class at his heels.

3. FRIEND OR FOE

I WORKED EXTRA HARD IN BASKETBALL practice that afternoon. I wanted to forget about Zell Starr even though his name was on the lips of every girl on the basketball team and indeed the school. I wanted to be exhausted when I went home.

Kate came in late for practice. I had not seen her since this morning.

"Where have you been all day?"

"Well, you know I had lunch detention for Coach Coldheart, right? We were sitting in detention having a stare-off, and he told me to get that ugly look off my face. Of course, you know me. I couldn't let that pass. I told him at least I could get ugly off my face, but if ugly were bricks, he'd be the Great Wall of China. Needless to say, he doesn't appreciate my humor and gave me work detail. I've been picking up trash from the halls and campus all afternoon."

As if on cue, Coach Coldheart walked into the gym blowing his whistle for the scrimmage to begin. Kate looked over at Coach and blew him a kiss.

"Kate, stop before you get suspended."

"Ahh, deep down, that old goat likes me."

Somehow, I believed her. I believed sparring with Kate was the most interesting part of Coach Neely's day.

Practice ended early, and I headed straight home. I wanted to fix a quick dinner for my father, do my homework, fall into bed, and have a dreamless night, but Dad called on my way home. He told me that he had ordered pizza. I was relieved because I was really tired. I just wished I could sleep well at night. I was becoming exhausted because of my restless nights. I had nightmares just about every night.

Jon called while I was sprawled out on my bed eating pizza and doing my homework. I spent a few minutes talking to him before I began to yawn. My pizza slice was half-eaten and my homework half done, but I could not hold my heavy lids open. Despite my best effort, I fell asleep talking to Jon.

I awoke confused the next morning. I was under the covers, and my phone was on the night stand plugged in. I sat up in bed and looked about. I didn't even remember going to bed last night. The last thing I remembered was talking on the phone with Jon.

I threw back the covers and climbed out of bed. After a shower, I dressed quickly and walked over to the dresser to finish my homework that I had left undone last night when I fell asleep. My books were closed and neatly stacked next to my book bag. I opened my notebook to my homework assignment. I knew I had enough time to finish it before I had to leave for school. I pulled back the chair at my desk and sat down opening my book to the appropriate page. I found where I had left off, and I ran my finger down my homework page to where I stopped last night.

Confused, I opened my notebook and took out my homework paper. It was finished. I was sure that I had left half of it incomplete when I fell asleep. I sat there in a daze for several minutes trying to remember finishing my homework. I couldn't remember finishing it at all. I sighed putting my homework back in my notebook and began packing my book bag.

"Good morning, dear," my dad called as I walked into the kitchen.

"Morning, Dad," I answered walking over to him and giving him a quick hug.

"What can I fix you for breakfast," he asked me.

"I'll just have some toast. I'm not very hungry."

"Annie, you're getting thin. You need to try to eat more."

"I'll try, Dad, just not this morning ok?"

"Alright dear, I just worry about you. You look so tired."

"Ah, I'm just not sleeping very well. I'll take that toast to go. I want to get to school early."

Dad put three pieces of buttered and jellied toast in some plastic wrap and handed it to me along with a coffee mug filled with juice.

"Thanks, Dad," I kissed his cheek, and suddenly, I became emotional. "I love you, Dad." I whispered throwing my arms around him and giving him a quick hug before I turned and left the room.

"Love you Annie," Dad whispered back.

I climbed into the Tahoe with a feeling of dread, and I didn't know why. I reached for the wrapped up toast and took out a piece. I put it in my mouth and put my car into reverse. Slowly, I drove to school munching on my breakfast. I pulled into a parking spot and turned off the motor. I finished a second piece and put the third in my book bag. Maybe I would have it for lunch.

As I opened my door and climbed out a sleek, convertible sports car pulled in the place next to mine. Great! It was the stalker, Zell.

"Good morning, Annie," Zell said smiling.

"Hey," I answered unenthusiastically.

I headed for class, and Zell quickly caught up with me.

We walked for a couple of minutes in silence.

"You had toast and jelly for breakfast this morning didn't you?"

"Like it's any of your business. Are you stalking me at home now?"

"No," he laughed. "It just looks like grape jelly on your chin."

"Seriously?" I groaned.

"Seriously," Zell replied. "Look at me."

I stopped and turned facing him. He bent and peered into my face. He wiped a finger across my chin and held it up for my inspection.

"There love. You're as good as new."

"Thanks," I mumbled returning to my trudge toward class.

"Is everything ok Annie?"

"Yeah, everything is just swell," I grunted.

"Can I do anything for you?" Zell asked.

"Yeah, leave me alone," I replied sourly.

"Really?"

"Yeah, really," I answered walking off and leaving him staring at my back.

I thought first period would never end. Every time I looked up, Zell was watching me. It began to unnerve me. When class was over, I jumped up and stomped to his chair before he got up.

"Stop watching me," I demanded.

"Why?" Zell asked.

"Because you're giving me the creeps."

"I apologize love. I never meant to upset you."

"I'm not your love." I stalked off leaving Zell still sitting in his seat. I'm not sure why I was in such a rotten mood today, but I was.

I could feel Zell watching me at lunch and in every class for the rest of the day, but I could not catch him in the act. He did as I asked and left me alone. Every time I felt his gaze, I would turn to him, and he would just be looking down at his paper, his hands, or a book. Even so, I knew he had been watching me just before I turned.

Finally, the day was winding down, and it was time for basketball practice. Kate and I walked together toward the gym.

"Boy, did you notice Zell today?" Kate asked.

"No, not really, why?"

"He looks so hot today," Kate purred.

"I'm not interested in Zell."

"He sure looks interested in you. At lunch, he couldn't take his eyes off you even though he was sitting at a table with five girls."

"Good. Maybe they will keep him busy, and he will leave me alone."

"Do you wanna go get a burger after practice?" Kate asked changing the subject.

"Yeah, that sounds good. I'll call Dad as soon as practice is over and let him know. I don't want to stay out long though. I want to go home, take a hot shower, and go to bed. I've been in a rotten mood today, and I'm not sure why. I think I'm tired, and I just want the day to be over."

"Tomorrow will be a better day," my loyal friend replied.

"I sure hope so," I sighed.

My evening went just as planned except I stayed up later than expected fussing over what I would wear to school tomorrow. I hoped that breaking from my dull dressing routine would cheer me up. I was the ultimate tomboy. I rarely wore anything but jeans and a tee-shirt, and here I was contemplating wearing a dress to school tomorrow. Why was I doing this? Even though I didn't want to admit it, I knew it was because of Zell. Even though he was impossibly attractive and stylish, I sensed an old-fashioned way about him. He spoke so properly and treated everyone so respectfully. He just seemed to be from another era. Of course between his impeccable manners and his impossible good looks, he had every girl and female staff member in school eating out of his hand. I was in a conundrum. Even though I wanted Zell to leave me alone, I still wanted him to notice me and think me attractive. I was being ridiculous, and I knew it.

I finally decided on a pretty, flowing spring skirt, a soft tank top, and lightweight cashmere sweater of the same pastel shade as the top. I picked a pair of sandals that would pick up an accent color in the skirt from the dozens of pairs in the closet. When at last I lay down, I was too troubled to sleep. I felt bad for being so rude to Zell today. It was uncharacteristic for me to be impolite to anyone. I needed to apologize to Zell tomorrow. I had barely looked at Zell today, but all I had heard all day was how hot he looked. I couldn't wait to get to school the next day to see if he was as unbelievably handsome as everyone was saying, or if we all just had an overactive reaction to the new guy in school. Then, there was art class. What happened there? Was it all a dream? It seemed real to me, too real. I was not entirely convinced what had happened during the video in art class had been a dream.

Finally, I drifted off to sleep. It seemed as though I had only been asleep for a few minutes when I awoke suddenly. I thought someone had touched me. My eyes slowly adjusted to the dark and focused on someone standing in the corner of my bedroom. Frightened, I fumbled for the switch to turn on the lamp beside my bed. As the light flooded the room, I could see that no one was there. I must have been dreaming again. I was probably just imagining everything, but here in my room, in the middle of the night, I was not so sure anymore. Anything seemed possible. My thoughts immediately went to Zell. Perhaps, he was a not the good guy he seemed to be. There was definitely something off about him just showing up in Dacula, Georgia saying he knew me. Perhaps, he is a psychopath like Ted Bundy, nice on the eyes, but having the heart of a killer. My blood ran cold, and I shivered. Sleep was almost impossible.

I was nervous the next morning. I washed my hair over and over again to make it shine. I even rolled it on a few electric rollers. The last time I rolled my hair was the previous spring for junior-senior prom. I must be losing my mind, but I could not stop. I was out of control. I was dressing for someone who may not give me the time of day especially since I was someone else's girlfriend. Nothing I did makes sense to me anymore. I carefully put on make-up so that my complexion was smooth and even. My hands shook as I made toast for breakfast. Even with the elaborate dressing ritual that I had just performed, it was still too early to leave for school.

Dad walked in the kitchen and jumped back startled dropping the paper he had just retrieved from the sidewalk.

"Annie, I didn't expect you in the kitchen so early. You surprised me," Dad said adjusting his glasses. "Is it picture day at school?" he added noticing that I was not in jeans and a tee-shirt.

Dad didn't intrude much in my life. His faith had been his profession and family since my mom died. I think he was afraid of attachment. I think he was fearful that he would lose me too and have his heart shredded once more. The only time I have seen him cry was the day my mother died in the accident. I had been thrown from the car and survived. Sometimes in those early years of her death, I would catch him looking at me strangely. I often thought he must wonder why I didn't die instead of her. I was almost a mirror image of my mother. My mother wore her hair short, so I wore mine long. She was so beautiful that she never wore make-up, so I did. She was a real Beaver Cleaver's mom. You know, she vacuumed wearing pearls, so I was the biggest tomboy ever. Not because I didn't want to look like my mom, but I did it for my dad's sake. The less I reminded him of her, the happier he seemed to appear. I knew it must rip his heart out every time he looks at me because I could have been her clone.

"You look beautiful, dear," he complimented me nervously adjusting his glasses again. My dad had trouble showing emotion. Emotional issues made him a basket case. He wasn't that way before she died. He had shriveled up emotionally after Mom's death.

I missed my mother. I was terrified of forgetting her. I had to keep a picture of her by the bed in my room to remind myself of what she looked like. I had been only five years old when she died. I still remember her smell and the way she felt when she held me in her arms, but her memory was fading.

"No, it's not picture day. I just felt like dressing up," I said reaching up on tiptoes to kiss his cheek. "I'm headed out for school. I want to get there early today. There's a new guy at school who is in all my classes, and he sits by me without fail. I want to get there early enough to make sure he doesn't get a seat close to me."

"This young man is not harassing you, is he?"

"No, he's just new and very popular, and it's a big distraction." I hurried from the kitchen and picked up my book bag from the table beside the door that led to the garage where my car was parked. It had taken a lot of persuasion to convince my dad to let me buy a car and drive. Old fears from my mother's death crowded our lives and made it difficult for him to accept the fact that I was growing up. Growing up meant that I would leave one day, and he would be alone.

Dad had taken the life insurance money he received from my mother's death and put it in a trust fund for me. Every month, a few hundred dollars were put into an account for me to use until my 21st birthday when I would receive the rest if I wanted. I appreciated having money of my own. That fact allowed me to play sports and not have to work a part-time job after school or constantly bug my father for money. It was also responsible for the dozens of pairs of shoes in my closet.

Hitting the remote to open the garage door, I threw my book bag in the passenger side of the car and walked around to the other side of the car. Hoisting myself into the driver's seat, I crammed my keys in the ignition and put the SUV in reverse. Seconds later a loud crash made me stomp my right foot on the brake. I looked in the rear-view mirror and groaned. I backed into a silver convertible sports car. Through the rear-view mirror, I couldn't tell what kind it was, but I could tell it looked very, very expensive. Throwing open the door of my vehicle, I jumped out of the car and walked toward the car that I just backed into. I stopped dead in my tracks when I saw who sat behind the wheel. It was Zell.

"What are you doing in my driveway?" I yelled at him.

"I thought we might ride to school together," he explained smiling.

"Oh noooo," I groaned as I walked to the front of his car and noticed the broken headlight and huge dent in his fender. "Look at your car," I said spreading my arms imitating the scope of the damage.

"It's just a car," Zell replied nonchalantly.

"Just a car," I squeaked. "It's a gorgeous car, and it looks incredibly expensive."

"Expense is relative," he said shrugging his shoulders.

"Relative to what?" I shouted horrified.

"I guess it's relative to what you can afford. I can afford to buy a dozen of these and not notice it in my bank account. Would you like this one?" he asked.

"Are you insane?" I screeched. "My dad would never let me drive this car. It's too fast and too small. Only a Sherman tank is good enough for me according to my dad."

"Well now," Zell said lightly as he joined me at the front of his car and surveyed the damage. "I suppose you will have to give me a ride to school."

"It's only a broken headlight and a dent, a rather enormous one, but still just a dent. Your car is drivable," I argued.

"Yes, but will you follow me to the body shop near the school and give me a lift? I can't stalk you with only one headlight." Zell laughed at the expression on my face when he said that.

"I will leave it there to be repaired, and you can be my chauffeur until I get it back," he explained grinning at me mischievously.

"Are you a psycho?"

"Yesterday you called me a creep and a stalker. Then today the morning has barely begun, and you call me a psycho. If I wasn't so incredibly well-adjusted, my self-esteem would be shattered," Zell said trying to look hurt.

"Just get in the car and cut the crap. I'll follow you," I sighed exasperated.

"By the way, you look lovely," he whispered drawing close to me.

"Yeah, I bet you say that to all the girls who crash into your car at 7:00 o'clock in the morning," I replied as I turned away from him, climbed in my car, and slammed the door.

I followed Zell to the repair shop and waited while he went inside to talk to the owner of the shop. While he was inside, I took a closer look at his car.

OMG, he was driving a Lamborghini. I didn't know what one cost, but I knew it probably cost him more than my dad paid for our house. I really felt crappy now.

I was all apologies when Zell returned to the car. "I'm so sorry that I was rude to you yesterday. I've been really tired lately, and I guess I took it out on you. I'm rarely rude to anyone. You didn't deserve to be treated that way, and I want to formally apologize."

"No worries," Zell said kindly and smiled at me.

"And I want to apologize about your car. I'm so sorry about wrecking it. I didn't know you drove such an expensive car. Why *do* you drive such an expensive car anyway?" I asked abruptly getting personal.

"It was for sale," he answered shrugging his shoulders.

"Are your parents rich?" I asked pursuing the question in my mind of how a high-school senior could afford a Lamborghini.

"Something like that. Annie, could you stop at the deli down from the school?" Zell asked changing the subject.

"Sure," I said as I put my tank in reverse and slowly pulled out into traffic.

The deli in question was more of a self-service station with a snack bar inside. A few booths and tables filled an addition to the building. In the mornings, they served bagels, biscuits, muffins, coffee, and juice.

I let Zell out and remained in the car looking at my face in the rear-view mirror. I seemed to be getting dark circles around my eyes from my restless nights. He returned a few minutes later with a couple of homemade cinnamon rolls, two bottles of orange juice, and fifteen red roses.

"These are all the roses they had," he apologized handing them to me. I knew that the store kept them in a vase by the register and charged about five dollars each for them.

"Why did you buy me roses?" I asked shocked.

"Take it as an apology for being in the wrong driveway at the wrong time," he quipped handing me a bottle of juice and a cinnamon roll.

"But we're on the way to school. They will die in the car during the day," I moaned suddenly sad that Zell's gift would be short-lived.

"We have plenty of time before school starts. Let's run back by your house and put them in a vase," he offered.

I looked at my cell phone. We still had forty-two minutes before the bell rang. Forty-two minutes would be plenty of time to make a quick trip back home and still get to school on time. I handed the roses back to Zell and put the car in reverse. When I pulled into our driveway, Dad was just backing out into the street. He stopped alongside my car and rolled down the window.

"Is something wrong?" he asked confused as to why I had come back home.

"No, nothing's wrong. It's a long story. I'll tell you about it tonight," I explained.

"Ok, if you're sure nothing is wrong," he said concerned.

"Everything's fine. I just need to run in the house a minute," I assured him.

"Bye then," he answered rolling up his window and pulling down the street.

I leaned over to retrieve the roses from Zell. "I'll be back in a minute."

I ran for the house being careful not to jostle the roses. Inside, I rummaged through the cupboards looking for a vase. I had never received flowers from anyone, but I thought that my mother had a crystal vase somewhere. I moved to the formal dining room and spied the vase inside my mother's China cabinet. I was filling the vase with water when I felt someone behind me. I turned to see Zell close behind me watching me. I didn't know if it was fear or excitement at being alone in the house with him, but I began shaking.

"You could've stayed in the car. I'll only be a minute," I told him.

"I like watching you," he replied.

When he said that, I didn't know whether to be frightened or delighted. My thoughts went back to last night and all the terrible suspicions that I had about Zell. Now, here I was all alone with him in my home. My heart started beating frantically. To hide my feelings, I busied myself arranging the roses in the vase. I carried them to the table in the entry foyer. A big mirror hung from the wall behind the table. The roses looked beautiful on the table, and their beauty was reflected in the mirror. Not bad for convenience store roses, and they were my first ever bouquet. I could tell by the reflection in the mirror that Zell was again standing behind me. I stood for several seconds looking in the mirror watching Zell watch me. I turned around to face him.

"Thank you. They are lovely," I said softly looking up into his face trying not to reveal this strange mixture of fear and gratitude that washed through me. "No one has ever given me roses before."

"I thought you would have received dozens of roses by now. Still, no rose has ever been as lovely as you," he replied moving close and looking into my eyes. Gently, he lifted my hand and pressed my palm to his cheek. For a brief moment, he closed his eyes and smiled. I felt as though my legs were melting. He moved my hand to his mouth and kissed the back of it. Still holding my hand, he slowly pulled me to him and held me tight against him for several minutes.

"Don't be afraid, Annie. I only came by this morning because I want to get to know you. I want us to be good friends. I thought I would offer you a ride to school. I don't guess my plan worked very well." Then, as abruptly as this little romantic interlude began, it stopped.

Still holding my hand, he pulled me to the door. "Biology calls," was all he said. I breathed a sigh of relief and locked the door. I stood quietly for a moment facing the door trying to still my racing heart. When I turned around, he stood holding open the passenger-side door for me. When I looked puzzled, "If you don't mind, I'll drive. I can afford the ticket," he laughed. He was right. If the police could have seen the blur that was my car, he would have received a ticket. I have never seen anyone drive so fast in my life. I felt as though I were a passenger in a car at the Daytona 500. He smoothly and deftly passed every car between us and Mill Creek High School. We actually pulled into the parking lot with ten minutes to spare. My heart felt as though it had sunk to the pit of my stomach though not from the drive back to school. I wouldn't admit it to Zell, but that ride was exhilarating. It had sunk because there in the parking lot stood Jon.

"Oh no," I groaned.

"What's wrong," Zell asked following where my eyes were fixated. "Oh," he said when he saw the object of my distress. He uttered a low, guttural laugh when he saw Jon's face grow a deadly crimson as he saw us.

"I don't need this drama," I said angrily throwing open the door and hopping out before Zell came to a complete stop. Jon came around to my side of the vehicle and propped his right arm against the top of my car blocking my way.

"I'm in a hurry." I murmured trying to push past him.

"Why is that guy driving your car?" questioned Jon furiously.

"Someone ran into his car, and I offered him a ride to school," I explained leaving out the fact that *I* was the one who backed into Zell's car in *my* driveway. I thought that fact was best overlooked at present.

"Why is that guy driving your car," Jon asked a second time just as angrily.

"He thought if he drove, he could get us to school on time, and he did," I tried to explain. "You know what a slow poke I am behind the wheel."

"Annie, we need to get to biology," Zell interrupted from behind me. He had come around the back of my car and was now standing behind me facing Johnny.

"Annie's not going anywhere with you," Jon popped off.

"He's right Jon. I missed a biology test this week. I can't be late today. I have to make up that test."

"Come on," Jon growled, "I'll walk you to class." He grabbed my elbow and jerked me forward. Instantly, Zell was in his face.

"If Annie wants you to walk her to class, that's fine, but don't ever grab her like that again," Zell warned his voice menacing.

"You don't tell me what I can do with my girl," Jon growled. They were nose to nose. The whole scene was interrupted by the ringing of the tardy bell.

"That's just great. Thanks a lot Jon," I yelled to him as I took off running toward the science wing as fast as sandals and a skirt would allow. I looked back once, and Zell and Jon were still nose to nose in a standoff—so much for male testosterone.

Dr. Patty was just getting around to roll call when I burst in the room. Every head in the room turned looking at me. Dr. Patty paused in calling the roll. For the second time this week, every student in class was looking at me in amazement mouths open in surprise. For many long seconds, no one moved; they just stared. I realized then that I was a bit more overdressed that normal. Dr. Patty called my name next on the roll. It appears that I made a grand entrance just in the nick of time.

"Anna Hayes, nice outfit," Dr. Patty said good-naturedly.

"Thank you," I murmured hurrying to my seat. I had no more than slithered into my seat when Zell entered the room. There was an audible gasp from some of the girls in class when he entered the room. He strode to a seat available at my lab table. Every head in class turned watching him. He was gorgeous as he glided toward my table. His hair was loose and moving around his incredible face as he walked in my direction. He had on a white tunic-like shirt that set off his deeply tanned face. Silver stars studded the hem of the untucked shirt that flowed bellowing out just below the silver belt of his gray jeans. I had never seen jeans of that color before. They looked incredibly expensive, and they fit like a glove. A pair of deep gray sandals adorned his feet today instead of the Italian leather shoes he wore yesterday. He was so masculine and sexy you could audibly hear the girls in the class sigh as he drifted past them. For someone that large, he was wonderfully graceful. I could not tear my eyes from him as he quickly covered the space between Dr. Patty and my lab table.

"Are you well?" he said quietly as he sat down across from me.

"Yes, I made it in time before Dr. Patty called my name on the roll," I whispered back. "What happened between you and Jon?"

"Nothing happened. As soon as his audience, namely you, left, so did his courage. He just walked off."

"I'm relieved," I sighed.

"I don't like him, Annie."

"Jon's a good guy, really. He just feels a bit threatened by you; I think."

"He should feel a lot threatened," Zell retorted.

"What do you mean by that?" I asked in a rather loud whisper causing several people at our lab table to look in our direction.

"Just this. I intend to take you away from him," Zell said seriously leaning over the table until he was only inches from my face.

"Jon and I have been friends for a long time," I argued.

"Fine, he can stay your friend. I want you as my girl."

In shock, I recoiled from him a bit. "Shhh, someone will hear you," I whispered.

"I don't care who hears."

"Well, I do. Jon will be furious. He'll kill me."

"No, he will not. In fact, he will never lay a hand on you again," Zell hissed.

"I was speaking figuratively, not literally. Calm down," I urged. "Why me? There are plenty of girls in school that are more attractive than I am. The lovely Leeann for one . . . "

"I have loved you for thousands of years," Zell cut me off hissing back at me. "I could never be interested in anyone else."

"I know it's been a few months since last summer when you *said* you met me, but thousands of years is hyperbole at its finest."

Dr. Patty arrived at our table as if on cue cutting off any further discussion to pass out our lab assignments. Thankfully, Zell was paired to work with Matthew since they were together on the other side of the table, and I was paired with Lauren, the smartest girl in class. I breathed a sigh of relief. I knew Lauren would take charge, and all I had to do was mindlessly follow her lead. I turned my back to Zell.

"Lauren, Jon and I can't wait until this weekend for your party." I chattered brightly looking out of the corner of my eye to see if Zell had heard my remark. If he did, there was no reaction. Lauren and I chattered continuously about boys and her party while we worked on our assignment. Take that Zell.

At the end of class, Zell stood waiting on me as I gathered my books and papers. "Stop waiting on me. I can't be seen with you between every class. The word will get back to Jon," I said nervously.

"Good," Zell stated flatly, "the sooner the better."

I looked at him letting out a moan of exasperation and huffed off around him. Zell followed behind, and when a gap in the crowd emerged, he quickly moved to my side.

"You can follow me around if you like, but I'm Jon's girlfriend. Please get that through your thick skull. I am his girl not yours!" I added with much more emphasis than I really felt.

"Not for long. You are my destiny," Zell remarked moving in front of me and stopping my forward movement.

When he said that, time seemed to stand still. People froze in their movement through the hall. I looked furtively up and down the hall in which everyone seemed to be moving in ultra-slow motion. The only two people that did not appear comatose seemed to be the two of us. Destiny—he echoed the sentiments that I had been feeling for a long time. Was this incredible young man my destiny? No, I refused to believe that. My destiny did not revolve around *any* guy, but yet when he said that it was as though pieces of my great puzzle were falling into place.

"Don't be ridiculous. I don't even know you," I growled.

"Yes, you do Annie. Please remember," Zell begged.

"Remember what? Even though you say we met in Europe, I have never seen you before yesterday. I would remember meeting someone like you."

"What do you mean someone like me?"

"I mean that I would remember meeting someone who looks as strange as you do?"

"I'm strange looking?"

"Yeah, total freak show material," I grumbled.

Zell narrowed his eyes and stared at me.

"Yeah, I bet you have a tin foil hat that you wear around at home, and you order Happy Meals with extra Happy." I huffed back at him.

Zell looked confused for a few moments, and then he began to smile. His smile turned into a laugh, and it became infectious. I began to laugh too.

"See I told you, extra Happy."

"Seriously Annie, we have known each other for a long time."

"I don't know you," I ceased to laugh and crossed my arms staring him dead in the face.

"Yes, you do," Zell said his laughter dying also.

"You're very badly mistaken!" I said louder than I meant to say it. People were slowing down in the hall to watch our altercation. "Oh, come on then. Walk with me." Letting him walk me to class was better than drawing attention to us. Besides, I knew Jon was on the other side of the campus this period.

"Jon and I have been dating for almost two years, and I can't just walk down the hall with you between every class and sit with you in every class."

"Is it serious between you two?" Zell's face suddenly turned ominous as we walked. I was sure that he was trying to read the emotions on my face.

I gave a short laugh. "If he had his way, it would be a serious relationship."

"I know," Zell answered deep in thought.

"What do you mean you know? This is your third day on campus," I retorted irritated that he was getting into my personal life.

"I just mean that I know if I was him, I would want a serious relationship with you too." Zell answered. Contrary to what he said, I had the feeling that was not at all what Zell meant. I was spooked all over again with the feeling that Zell knew more about me than was humanly possible.

Coach Hatcher was on the computer when we entered the classroom. Zell took my arm and guided me to a couple of desks in the back corner.

"How do you even fit in those things?" I asked him as he struggled to sit in the too small desk.

"I much prefer the tables in biology and art," Zell joked standing with the desk attached dangling from around his waist. Matthew sat to the right of me and laughed loudly. He tried to cover the laugh with a coughing fit when I turned to glare at him.

"Please don't encourage him," I remarked dryly to Matthew.

Zell impressed everyone as he answered question after question that Coach Hatcher asked in Calculus.

"Who are you?" Coach Hatcher called to him wrinkling his brow.

"That is exactly the same question I have been asking, and he refuses to tell me which planet he comes from," I said aloud shocked at my bold statement. The class broke out in laughter, and Coach Hatcher gave me a stern look. I wilted.

"Zell Starr, new student."

"Oh yeah, new student," Coach Hatcher mumbled. "Welcome to Mill Creek High."

"Thank you, sir."

Matthew leaned across the aisle and muttered to me, "What's with all the manners?"

"I told you he was from outer space," I sighed and raised my hands as if resting my case. Confident that I had been vindicated, I pulled out a nail file and began filing a nail.

"What kind of name is Zell Starr anyway? Mongolian or something?" I asked tartly. Why was I behaving this way? I spent an hour planning what to wear the next time I saw him, and here I was insulting him.

"Zell, short for Zazel, and Starr, from whence I came, the stars. You did call me an alien, correct?" he laughed at his own joke throwing my previous comment back in my face.

Glad that he was not taking offense at my insults, I began to smile back at him, but at the mention of his name, Zazel, something tugged at my memory. I *had* heard that name before. A look of panic crossed my face, and I caught his eyes as I abruptly looked up. I didn't know where or when, but I knew at that moment that he was telling the truth. We had met before. My brow wrinkled as I tried to recall where I had met him. It was no use. I couldn't remember. All I knew was that he had spoken truthfully when he said he knew me. I looked at the profile of his face as he turned and gazed ahead listening to Coach Hatcher.

Jeez, he was handsome. I had never believed in reincarnation, but I was beginning to think maybe we had been a couple in a previous life. I could not stop staring at him. He must have felt my stare and turned his perfect head to smile at me. Stop it. You have a boyfriend. I repeated again to myself; I have a boyfriend. Stop smiling at him. Stop. But, I couldn't. I was losing the battle. That must be the reason for my sharp tongue. I was too attracted to him. Maybe, I was subconsciously trying to make him hate me. If he hated me, I was safe. My dull, drab life was safe. Everything would return to normal.

When the bell rang, Zell laid his books on top of mine and picked them all up as if it were nothing. Those books must weigh fifty pounds, and he picked them up with one hand easily. He guided me through the door and hall to the big art classroom at the end of the corridor. Placing our books on an art table, he pulled a chair out for me.

"I can't sit with you in every class," I protested.

"Why not?" Zell asked perplexed.

"Because I have a jealous boyfriend," I replied through clenched teeth.

"I'm not jealous at all," Zell laughed.

"You are not my boyfriend," I stated flatly.

"Yes, I am. It's just a matter of time before you admit it."

"You are psychotic," I said as loud as I dared. "I have a boyfriend, and you're not him."

Zell reached over and ran the tips of his fingers around my hand tracing my fingers with his.

"Don't touch me," I hissed.

His eyes met mine and locked there. I saw a small smile tug at the corner of those beautiful lips. I felt that warm knot return to my stomach. I was doing my best to shake it off when the bell rang. I thought art would never end. Ms. Picknell must be home recovering from the field trip because she was out again today. A sub gave the class worksheets to complete. Thank goodness there was not another video! I turned my back to Zell and refused to look at him the rest of class.

"Thank God," I breathed in a loud sigh of relief when the dismissal bell rang.

Zell was standing before me holding my books before I could reach for them.

"What did God do?" he asked innocently.

"Just give me my books and leave me alone," I said hatefully.

Zell didn't seem hurt at all. He laid our books down on the closest desk and pulled me in his arms.

"Why are you so catty with me?"

"Catty?" I laughed.

"Yes, catty."

"Because."

"Why?" Zell asked moving only inches from my lips.

"It's easier that way."

"What is easier?"

"It's easier to be mean to you than to fall for you."

"Annie," he whispered pulling me close and kissing my cheek. Everyone in class froze in place staring at us.

"You'll be dead when Johnny hears about this," I stood on my tip-toes and got as close as I could to his eyes and threatened him.

Zell sighed, "Really, Annie. You think Jon is capable of terminating my life?"

"Why do you talk that way? 'Terminating my life, catty?' I gasped. I was beginning to feel weak and shaky.

"You are being dramatic, Annie."

"I don't even **know** you, and if you don't want drama, then just leave me alone,"

"But you will," Zell said exasperated, "remember me if you'll let yourself. I'm only trying to help you remember."

"Humph." I snorted and wrenched myself out of his arms, but my legs started to wobble. "What have you done to me?" My hands were shaking, and I could not think straight.

Zell caught me before I hit the floor.

"Please Annie, behave before I have to kiss you again," Zell threatened in a low voice.

I gasped, "You wouldn't dare."

"Try me," Zell answered grimly hovering over me.

My lips went into a grimace hiding my lips from Zell.

"Do you really think that will work if I want to kiss you?" Zell whispered in my ear.

Keeping my lips pressed together, I glared at him. No one in class moved. Everyone was watching and listening to us.

"I think you are still ill Annie and need to go home. I'm going to take you to the office."

"I'll scream if you come near me," I ground out between clenched teeth and lips, my body beginning to shake uncontrollably.

"I don't think you will," Zell threatened.

"How do you figure that?"

"Because here comes your future ex-boyfriend," Zell said smiling.

"Good grief," my heart sank to my stomach. Zell still had his arm around my waist supporting me.

"Are you going to be a good girl, or are we going to make out in front of your ex?" Zell laughed apparently enjoying himself. The bell had rung, but still no one moved watching the exchange between Zell and me.

Jon burst through the door pausing to search the room. He found me looking into Zell's face while Zell held me up with one arm. Panic-stricken, my head snapped around to meet Jon's glare. The rage on his face suddenly made me frightened. His normally tanned complexion was white with anger. He crossed the room in large strides stopping at my side with his eyes fixed on Zell's arm that circled my waist holding me close to him. Everyone turned to watch the fight that they were sure was about to happen.

"Annie, what is going on? People have been telling me that you and this guy have been together all morning," Jon yelled glaring at Zell.

"I don't think we have been formally introduced," Zell said and stuck out his hand attempting to shake Jon's hand. "Annie and I just have the same classes, and she has been kind enough to show me around."

Jon ignored the outstretched hand and waited for me to answer.

Zell and Jon were nose to nose staring in each other's eyes. Neither one was willing to back down. I didn't understand what happened next. One second they were nose to nose. The next Johnny was looking up into Zell's eyes. One second, they were the same height. The next, Zell is three or four inches taller. That fact seemed to take Jon by surprise too. He took a step back blinking.

"I, um, I um, don't know . . . ," I tried to answer but the swimming in my head returned with a vengeance making my legs about as sturdy as cooked pasta. Swaying again, my knees crumpled beneath me.

Zell scooped me up in his massive arms before I hit the floor.

"Excuse us," Zell told Jon gracefully sidestepping around him. "Annie doesn't seem to be well." He strode purposefully from the classroom with me cradled in his arms before Jon could respond. The door slammed behind us as we left. Never, if I live to be one hundred will I forget the look of shock and rage on Jon's face as Zell carried me from the classroom. Jon tried to follow, but the door was stuck. The substitute teacher picked up the phone to the office and asked for someone to send the custodian to the room to fix the faulty door.

Zell walked down the hall still holding me like a child in his arms. He stopped by the office on his way out of the school to tell Mrs. Woods that I was unwell, and he was taking me home. Mrs. Woods opened her mouth to argue, but took one look at me cradled in Zell's arms and shook her head. I wanted to argue, but the sleepless nights were beginning to take their toll. I felt exhausted and could barely keep my eyes open.

Zell put me in the passenger side of my Tahoe and buckled the seat belt. Sliding into the driver's side, he put the car into reverse. Smoothly, the vehicle backed from the parking space. Even more smoothly, he navigated through the crowded parking lot and on to the highway. That is the last thing I remembered as a dark cloud overtook me.

4.   THE ISLAND

WHEN I REGAINED CONSCIOUSNESS, I WAS lying in an overstuffed lounge chair overlooking a calm, sparkling lake with a sheer bluff of rock behind me.

"Where am I?" I squeaked.

"You're with me at my home," Zell answered quietly.

"Are your parents at home?" I asked.

"My mother has long been dead," Zell replied quietly with a sad faraway look in his eyes. "My father, well . . . who knows, chained in a pit somewhere maybe."

"You're kidding, right?" I questioned.

"No, not really," Zell replied not looking at me.

"How does a high-school student afford a place like this?" I asked sweeping my hands toward the mansion perched at the base of the bluff. "How does DFACS allow a minor to live alone?"

"Annie, I think we both know that I am not a minor."

"Then let's back up to question number one. How does a high-school student afford a place like this?"

"I think we both know I'm not really a normal high-school student either."

"What are *you* exactly, then?"

"I don't think you're ready for the truth yet, Annie."

"What is the big mystery with you? Who are you really?" I pushed him for an answer.

"Can't it be enough for now for us to be together?" he sighed turning to look at me.

"Not for me. I never said I wanted to be here with you. I think the authorities would call this kidnapping," I said snidely. "I need to go back to school. I have basketball practice. "

"It's after five o'clock. I think you slept through most of it."

"Just exactly how did you drug me? I've heard of guys slipping drugs in a girl's drink, but I wasn't drinking anything."

"I've never even taken an aspirin Annie. I would never do anything to harm you. I don't think you could handle it if I told you."

"Try me," I ordered.

"If I tell you, will you try to be nice to me?" Zell looked sadly into my eyes. "I've come on a long, hard journey just to be near you."

"You could have saved yourself the trip." I spat back, but I was immediately sorry when I saw the pain and sadness my words caused in his eyes.

"All right. All right. I'll be nice if you answer three questions for me."

"Will you stop dating Jon if I answer all three?" Zell bargained cracking a half smile.

I took out my cell phone and pretended to dial 911.

"Yes, officer, this is Annie Hayes. Could you send a car to the mansion of Zell Starr out on Lake Lanier? He has drugged me, kidnapped me, and no one seems to know who he is or where he came from."

"OK, Annie, but you may not like what I have to tell you. I didn't drug you. I just kissed your cheek. I had no idea it would affect you in the manner that it did. I think you may be exhausted, and your exhaustion caused my kiss to be more potent."

"I don't sleep very well," I agreed.

"I know," Zell replied quietly.

"What do you mean you know?" I lay my phone beside me ending my pretentious call. When he didn't answer, I decided just to ask him a few questions and go home.

"Question number one: Who are *you* exactly? Don't tell me Zell Starr, transfer student, from some mysterious country in Europe either."

"I am Zazel, The Last of the Anak," Zell replied not looking at me. He sat with his hands intertwined as he gazed over the lake seemingly deep in thought.

"A What?" I asked incredulously wrinkling my brow.

Zell turned looking at me and smiled. "Not a What, an Anak, Annie."

"What then is an Anak exactly?" I asked not relenting. However, the sad look that crossed Zell's face earlier when he mentioned his mother did not leave his eyes.

"Have you ever heard of Fallen Angels?" Zell asked turning back to the lake not meeting my gaze.

He sat with a faraway look in his eyes as if remembering some ancient memory.

"Humph," I huffed, "I'm a preacher's daughter. I know those are the angels who rebelled against God and were thrown out of heaven."

"Yes, something like that," Zell murmured. "The Archangels cast them from heaven, and they fell to earth. The Fallen Angels or Watchers, of which my father, Azâzêl, was one, looked at the women of earth and desired them. The children born to the Fallen Angels and the human women, of which my mother was one, became a race of bloodthirsty giants."

Almost mechanically Zell began to speak as if he was reading some ancient text. 'And they became with child,' Zell said, 'and they bare great giants, whose height was three thousand ells. And when men could no longer sustain them, the giants turned against them and devoured mankind, and drank their blood. And Azâzêl taught men to make swords, and knives, and shields, and breastplates, and as men perished, they cried, and their cry went up to heaven. And then Michael, Uriel, Raphael, and Gabriel, the Archangels, looked down from heaven and saw much blood being shed upon the earth, and all lawlessness being wrought upon the earth. And they said to the Lord of the ages, Thou seest all things, and nothing can hide itself from Thee. Thou seest what Azâzêl hath done, who hath taught all unrighteousness on earth and revealed the eternal secrets which were (preserved) in heaven, and made known to men the metals of the earth and the art of working them. . .'

Zell turned to me, "Long story from an ancient text, the *Book of Enoch,* made short, the archangels Michael, Uriel, Raphael, and Gabriel went before God and asked him to do something about the giants who were killing mankind and my father, Azâzêl, who was teaching all of mankind how to make weapons from metal which was an eternal secret of Heaven and never intended for mankind. God turned the hearts of the Nephilim, or Anak, the giants, against one another, so they would exterminate themselves. I am from the race of the giants, the offspring between a human woman and a Fallen Angel. I have fought each of them that has come for me and won against each one. I am the last of the race, the race called the Anak, children of the Watchers. However, I have never been like the others. I hate what I am. I love God, and I have never shed the blood of the innocents. Conversely, I have spent my life protecting mankind hoping that God would forgive me my heritage and redeem me. I have longed for impossible things—to be human—to have you." Zell finished with a heart so heavy that I could feel his torment. He reclined back against the chair and buried his face behind his arms not finishing his sentence.

I sat in shocked silence trying to absorb everything Zell had just told me. After what seemed to be an eternity, Zell uncovered his face turning it to look into my eyes.

"Can you imagine what it feels like to be the only one of your kind? To wander the earth for thousands of years knowing you were soulless but still trying to save the world? You, Annie, have kept me going. I have known you for thousands of years before you were born. As a young man, I had a vision of you. I knew our destinies were intertwined. You are going to change the world. It is my job to protect you until your destiny is fulfilled, and it is my heart that will protect you even beyond the fulfillment of your destiny," Zell moved closer and whispered to me with such emotion that I almost believed what he spoke was true. Even though I believed he may believe that he was speaking truthfully, it was hard for me to think that I would ever do anything to change the world, even if I could get past his children of the corn story.

When my mother died, I was young, but it is still a memory that is burned into my mind. I still see my father standing at my mother's coffin crying. Even that was not sadness as deep as this sadness that Zell carried within his soul. He said he was without a soul, yet I found that hard to fathom. Even though he knew things about me that I couldn't explain, he never had done anything to harm me. He seemed so righteous and good. I reached out my hand and touched the part of his face that was not buried in his arms.

"Please don't be sad. You're breaking my heart," I whispered. The atmosphere between us was so emotionally charged that not meaning to, I rose and moved close to Zell. I put my arms around him, and l laid my head against his shoulder. Zell hesitated then turned in my arms. He wrapped his arms around me.

"Please don't hate me Annie. I could not bear it if you did. Mine has been the loneliest existence possible—waiting for someone not yet born. Not knowing, even when you were born, if I would ever find a way to reveal myself to you. Not knowing, if you would look upon me as a monster," Zell whispered into my ear.

"You are not a monster Zell. I don't hate you. Honest, I don't. I'm sorry that I have been rude to you, but I still cannot believe this story you have told me. I haven't believed in anything since my mother died. Maybe, I'm mad at God for taking her from me if He exists."

"Maybe it was not God who took her from you."

"What do you mean?" I asked.

"Ask me another question," Zell avoided answering my question.

"What happened at school today when you kissed my cheek?"

I saw the corner of Zell's lip turn up as he remembered the scene with Johnny.

"Annie, I'm sorry. I didn't know just kissing your cheek would do that to you. It seems that I have this effect on humans. If I kiss one, they have a reaction. Remember, I am one-half celestial. Humans tremble, shake, and seem to lose the ability to think and remember the event. It is only temporary, and there are no bad effects other than no memory of what has occurred. It seems to be a defense mechanism my body has; however, if I were you kiss you often enough, you most likely would build up a tolerance to me. The effects of my kiss would lessen. Should we work on your building up a tolerance?" Zell suggested his somber mood lifted, and he moved within centimeters of my lips smiling.

I huffed. "What do you mean humans? What else would you kiss?"

"Questions three and four," Zell shouted jumping up.

"That's not fair," I shouted back.

"All's fair in love and war," Zell quoted. "Come with me Annie. I want to show you something," Zell pleaded.

"Where do you want me to go?" I asked.

"It's some place very special," he replied reaching out and taking my hand.

"I don't know. I'm still not sure you are not a serial killer or whack job."

"Annie, one thing you can bet your life on is that I will never, ever harm you. I am here to protect you."

"Protect me from what?" I asked holding up my hands and looking around.

"I don't want to tell you. It will frighten you."

"I am not frightened. I don't buy into your fairy tale. You tell a good story, but don't expect me to believe it."

"Then come with me. It's Friday. There is no school tomorrow," Zell pleaded. "Please come."

The thought of spending a few more hours alone with Zell was terribly exciting though frightening, but I decided to bargain.

"If I come, I get my third question again," I said smugly laying out my terms.

"Deal," Zell agreed sticking out his hand for me to shake on it. I reached for his masculine hand and agreed. "Now, close your eyes, and don't be afraid. I am going to put my arms around you, but remain very still," Zell cautioned. "Do you promise?"

"Yes, yes, I promise." I groaned exasperated with his pleading. Zell moved behind me, and I sighed and leaned against him. I could feel Zell hesitate. Then he wrapped his arms around me. What happened next is still impossible for me to believe, but it happened. Of that, I am sure. Zell held me close, and we began to rise. My feet felt as though they had left solid ground as Zell held me close to his beating heart. I turned in his arms and looked up into his eyes. The sadness that had been there was evaporating. He gazed back into my eyes. I was distracted for a moment, lost in his handsome silver gaze until I was startled by a bird that flew close by, and I glanced in its direction. It was then that I noticed that we were far above his lovely home by the shore of Lake Lanier. It was growing smaller and smaller. We were airborne! I screamed clutching Zell to me. I could see strong, white and silver wings stretched toward the sky lifting us increasingly farther from the ground.

"Zell," I screamed.

"It's fine Annie. You're safe with me."

Frantically, I tightened my arms around Zell. "Let me go!"

Zell grinned back at me. "Are you sure you want me to let go of you?"

"No!" I screamed hysterically clutching at him.

I began to hyperventilate. Zell kissed me on the forehead, but that brief contact soothed me. My breathing became even.

"Don't worry. I won't let you fall," Zell reassured me. "I want to show you something."

"No, let's go back. I'm afraid. Someone may see us."

"No one can see us; we are moving much too fast for the human eye to keep up with. They will think we are just a cloud moving with the wind," Zell answered.

He was right. I could feel the speed with which we were moving, but he cradled me and protected me from the wind and force of gravity as we moved. Suddenly, I felt as if we were slowing and moving downward. Gently, we touched earth again, and I sighed deeply with relief tentatively opening one eye and then another.

It happened so fast. I barely noticed as the wings that had held me disappeared behind his back.

"What were those?" I asked fearfully.

"A gift from my father," Zell joked.

I meant to ask him more, but I looked around where we landed and could not believe my eyes.

We were in the middle of a body of water on a small secluded island. The island rose sharply from the water with steep bluffs on every side keeping even the most adventurous human from putting a foot on the island. There was a thin narrow, sandy beach that circled the island before the land climbed up the bluffs. Someone would need a helicopter to land there, or they would need Zell. The top of the bluff was a paradise. There were flowers of every color and description here. Everywhere, there were flowers. Even where there should have been grass, there was white and purple asylum that covered the soil like a carpet. On the far end, the bluff was higher, and as it fell back toward the plateau stones cascaded down piled one upon another making a beautiful waterfall. The pool at the base of the waterfall led to a larger waterfall that flowed over the bluff. This was the most beautiful sight I had ever seen.

"Oh Zell," I breathed softly, "This is exquisite."

"I'm glad you like it. It is for you."

"What are you talking about, for me?"

"I mean that I created this garden for you. I just hoped that someday I would be able to show it to you."

"But how did you create all this?"

"I can kill a great beast with only a sword. What kind of a challenge are a few flowers to me?" Zell laughed. He reached down and snapped the stem of a deep red rose in half. He pulled the thorns from the stem and gently ran the rose underneath my nose.

"Ummmm, that smells heavenly, but seriously," I replied not impressed with his humor. "How did this place come to be, and what beast are you speaking of?"

"I wanted a place where we could be totally alone, so I created one," Zell answered sweeping his hands out toward the landscape.

"You really created this place." I replied in wonder.

"Yes, for you." With that, Zell placed the rose in my hand.

"But you live alone already." I murmured quietly lifting the rose to my nose to inhale its fragrance again.

"I have a housekeeper and an assistant who runs the family business, and they, also, can pose as my mother and father when needed. They live on my property."

"I didn't see them."

"They are very discreet."

"Mmmm," I replied not knowing whether I answered him or was responding to the scent of the rose.

"How long did it take you to make it this beautiful place?"

"Only a hundred years or so."

"You're kidding, right?"

"No, I'm not. It was just a big rock in the middle of the ocean when I began," he answered.

"What did you mean when you said a minute ago that you could kill a great beast with only a sword?"

"Do you not remember what happened the night you left school late after basketball practice?" he asked.

"No, I tried to remember earlier, but I felt frightened and just stopped thinking about that night. I only remember waking up late the next morning."

We walked to the side of the island with the waterfall. I moved to a flat boulder that rested against the rock wall making a sort of natural chair and sat down to gaze toward the side of the island we had just come from. It was breathtaking. There were trees with long, limber branches like a willow, but were covered in violet and rose-colored blooms. Hydrangeas in hues of azure, purple, red, pink, and white grew expansively along a wall of bamboo. In front of the hydrangeas grew marigolds, petunias, dahlias, coneflowers, and multitudes of other flowers that must have been tropical because I was not familiar with them. In front of this row of flowers grew low growing, flowering border plants in white, blue, and purple. Zell sat on the carpet of flowers at my feet leaning against my calves and the rock upon which I sat. Shyly, I looked at his profile. He was unlike any young man that I had ever seen. There were no imperfections in his face or body. I looked at the smooth line of his jaw and wished I could run my fingertips along it.

I forced my hands to remain in my lap. I could not let myself fall in love with him. I have a boyfriend. I have a boyfriend. I have a boyfriend. I repeatedly recited this fact in my head to keep from touching Zell.

I looked at his back, and there was no evidence of wings. There were no bumps or any indication that his back had been a mass of wings.

As if I had spoken his name, Zell turned looking at me.

"Where are your wings?" I asked running my fingers over his smooth back.

"They are there."

"Where? I don't see or feel anything." I answered wondering if I was going mad. Wondering, if we had really just flown here, or if I was dreaming again.

"They are there."

"Where?"

"Let me see if I can explain this." Have you ever seen any of the older model sports cars whose headlights flip up when you turn on the lights?"

"Of course," I said sharper than I meant to be.

"When you turn off the headlights, they disappear back into the hood of the car. It is the same way with my wings. When I don't need them anymore, they disappear into my back."

"That is just too freaky."

"Freaky or not, it's part of my equipment," Zell said laughing at me.

"Zell, may I ask you another question?"

"Of course, anything."

"You spoke earlier of my destiny. What is my destiny?"

"You will know when the time comes. I have seen a couple of ways that this may be accomplished, but it is up to fate as to the events that come to pass. It is also up to you the path you actually take. You will change the world."

"Should I be frightened?"

"Yes," Zell answered honestly, "because of your destiny, you are hunted by the Dark Ones, but you have me. I will protect you with my life."

"So what do we do now?"

"We survive until it is your time," Zell stated flatly.

5. PARADISE

WE SAT THERE FOR A LONG TIME TALKING to each other and gazing at the garden. Finally, Zell stood up taking my hand and pulling me up with him.

"Come, I want to show you something."

Zell pulled me across the clearing to the bamboo forest where a stone trail disappeared into a thicket of bamboo skyscrapers. We followed the trail in silence. Zell held my hand and pulled me behind him. The path ended at another stone cliff where it widened into a clearing. Built into the stone cliff, there stood a small stone cottage. The flat, thick stones were stacked into sturdy walls. There were tiles of cedar on the roof. Zell saw me looking at the roof.

"I hewed those from actual Cedars of Lebanon. I thought they would give the cottage a rustic look."

"You built this cottage?"

"Yes, I told you it took me a hundred years or so to build this island for you. Of course, I didn't get to work on it every day. There have been a few Anak

[89]

to slay, Dark Angels to battle, and monsters to cut down to size every now and then. I somehow knew that you were only a century or two away from being born. I guess you could equate the mood that enveloped me to that of an expectant mother who knows her time is near and starts cleaning and preparing for her babe to be born. I was the same way. I was consumed with preparing a place for you both here and at the lake house. I haven't worked on either since the day you were born."

"The day I was born?" I echoed questioningly.

"Yes, once you were born, I have done nothing but protect you."

"Protect me?" I asked again dazed.

"Yes, the Dark Ones have hunted you from the day of your birth," Zell answered darkly.

"How is it that I have never seen you before?"

"Oh, but you have Annie," Zell replied taking my face in his large hands.

"I don't remember ever seeing you before your first day at school. However, I think I have dreamed of you," I whispered still staring past Zell at the cottage.

"Come, I want to show you inside." Zell put his arm around me deciding not to comment on my last remark.

Reluctantly, I went with him through a massive solid wood door. Of course, it would have to be massive for Zell to fit through.

"I couldn't wait any longer to show you our special place."

"Wait a minute, Zell. There is no 'our.' I have a boyfriend."

"Pshttt." Zell sputtered and waved his hand as if dismissing the thought.

"As I was saying,"

"Zell, I hate to interrupt you, but it is getting late. I have to get home."

"Why, tomorrow is Saturday?"

"My dad will be worried."

"No, he won't. I've already called him."

"What do you mean you've already called him?"

"I called him and told him you were staying at a friend's house tonight."

"What friend?" I asked.

"Your new friend, Starr."

"Wait a minute. My dad has never met you. Why would he believe anything you say?"

"I didn't say anything. You did."

"I did?"

"Yes, you."

"I am totally confused."

"Well, I must admit. I did sound like you when I called."

"Zell, what did you do?"

Zell shrugged his shoulders and smiled mischievously.

"Promise you won't be mad?" Zell asked.

"No, I don't promise anything."

"You have to promise, or I won't tell you."

"Zell!" I yelled, "Spit it out!"

"Promise me."

"No!" I stated emphatically.

"You're just going to have to trust me then when I say that your father is not expecting you," Zell said coolly moving over to an expansive sofa and sitting down.

"Zell, take me home now."

"No can do," Zell stretched out resting his massive arms on the back of the sofa.

"OK, I promise," I gave up the fight raising my hands in defeat.

"Oh, Annie, you gave up too easily," Zell laughed out loud.

I gave him a dark look. He laughed easily.

"Fine, fine, but remember you promised you won't be mad. Remember the day in class when I wrote your report in your handwriting?"

"Of course, I remember," I retorted not smiling and not knowing where this was going.

"I have this gift of being a perfect mimic. Possibly it's an angelic gift, but perhaps not. I don't know. I just know that I am an extraordinary mimic. When I called your dad this afternoon, I used your voice while you were still asleep. I couldn't take you home in that condition. I honestly didn't know how long it would take you to recover. I didn't want your dad to worry, or for you to get in trouble. I know it wasn't right, but it was the only solution that I could think of. This is all different for me too. I have rarely used *that* particular gift on anyone," Zell explained acting embarrassed that he had kissed me on the cheek at school and caused this whole dilemma. "I was trying to protect you. I pretended to be you and asked him if you could stay over at a new friend's house tonight named Starr. Your dad trusts you completely. He never hesitated to say yes. You have nothing to fear from me. I promise. I know it wasn't the right thing to do, but I couldn't take you home. I've dreamed of showing this place to you for so long. I understand though if you want to go home, I'll take you now," Zell finished and waited for my reaction. He was expecting the worst, and I think he was surprised when I calmly answered.

"I see," was all I could think to say. "I guess I can stay for a while since I've already cleared it through my dad," I said giving Zell a sour look. I had promised not to be angry, so I was trying hard not to be. I wandered back outside and took in the breathtaking beauty of the island, our island, and the serenity of it immediately soothed my anxiousness.

Besides, perhaps Zell was just trying to protect me and save my Dad from worrying about me. What did Zell have in mind for this evening though? Most of me didn't want to stay with him, but another part of me was excited at the thought of having Zell all to myself. Especially having him to myself on this beautiful island that according to him, he built for me before I was born. This was all too strange to be true. Should I be frightened? Was this person standing before me a sinister force? Could he possibly be who he says he is? Could he actually be over six thousand years old, but yet still not appear much older than me? He did fly us to this island without the help of a plane. His kiss, even those that barely qualify, reduces me to a quivering mess. Then there are the dreams and the nightmares that are so frightening. In them, someone was always there to protect me. Was it Zell? If I were honest, I believe I could remember him too in my earliest memories and dreams. We have just never spoken or touched until now.

"Annie?" Zell asked concerned at the faraway look in my eyes. "I'm sorry that I deceived your dad. I'll never do that again. I feel so guilty about it. I just couldn't take you home as you were. I didn't know how long the effects of my kiss would last. I just saw

Jon coming through that door after you, and I reacted badly. I admit that I wouldn't mind if he chose to break up with you, but it's not right embarrassing you or him with a crowd watching. I hope you'll forgive me. I'm not sure how the kiss works. I only used it on one other person, and she was many hundreds of years ago.

I felt a ridiculous pang of jealously, and I snapped back to reality to search Zell's face.

"She saw me in my Anak form. She screamed and screamed and screamed. I kissed her to stop her screaming, but she was unconscious for a week afterwards. That's why I called your dad. I thought you would be unconscious for at least a couple of days. You must be stronger than she was."

I breathed easier knowing his kiss was not a lover's kiss, but he meant to soothe the woman. I blinked a few times and tried to focus on his face.

"Possibly," I answered quietly.

"Are you angry with me?"

I shook my head slowly. "No, I promised I wouldn't be."

"What is it then?" Zell asked with a worried expression.

"I just . . . I just think that your kiss might have worked. It seems as if I remember you from a childhood memory," my voice trailed off as I seemed to go catatonic again.

Zell gathered me in his arms and held me close. Neither one of us said anything. Slowly, my arms left my side and slid around Zell's waist. He crushed me closer still and laid his head on the top of mine.

"Annie," Zell barely breathed my name. "If I die now, I die gladly now that I've held you in my arms. This moment—it's all I've ever dreamed of."

We stood like that until the sun began to fade outside. Finally, Zell took my hand and guided me into the cottage. He motioned for me to sit on the sofa in front of a stone fireplace that looked hundreds of years old and most likely was.

"I'll build a fire. The wind on top of this plateau is pretty cool after the sun goes down. That is why I planted the bamboo forest on the windward side of the island to break up the blow of the wind." Zell talked as he busily built a fire. "I'll fix you something to eat." He suddenly acted awkward and uncomfortable about the fact that we were truly here in the middle of the ocean, perched high atop impenetrable cliffs, utterly alone, just the two of us. He moved to a small kitchen area and took out a large steak which he cut into strips. He lightly browned the strips on top of a gas stove that looked incredibly modern and new. He quickly made a salad as the steak strips sizzled.

"A guardian angel that cooks?"

"I'm half human, remember. The best part of me is human. I understand why God loves you so. As a race, you are spectacular."

"I don't feel very spectacular at the moment. Tell me about your mother."

"She died in childbirth when I was thirteen years old."

"Did your father raise you after she died?"

"Humph," Zell snorted. "My father was only in and out my whole life. It was over a year after she died that he came back and found out she had died in childbirth."

"Did he stay with you then?"

"No. When he swept through the door asking for her, I told him she wasn't there that she, and my baby brother died during the birth. He stood still for a few moments looking into my face. Then he turned and left again without saying a word."

"How did you live? Who took care of you?"

"My mother's sister, my aunt, Miriam, looked after me somewhat. Her house was too crowded and small. I lived in my mother's house alone most of the time. Although, in the beginning, I usually showed up at Aunt Miriam's at meal times." Zell's serious tone was broken by soft laughter. "I had eleven cousins, each more mischievous than the last. That is when I learned to cook. Better to cook than to fight them over the meals." He laughed again at some faraway memory.

"Is that the last time you saw him?"

"No, when I was fourteen he came back again. I had just had my vision of you a few weeks before his return. He taught me how to fashion swords and the secret of the flaming sword. According to my father, he was teaching me a trade, so that I could support myself. I decided then and there that I would become your protectorate. That I would turn the only thing my father ever gave me, the knowledge to fashion weapons from metal and make a business of it. I vowed that I would perfect the swords and knives I made, and I would become the most skilled warrior the world had ever seen. I decided to wait for you and defend you even until death itself."

"The Archangels became upset that Azâzêl, my father, was teaching humans to make weapons. Not just me, he taught many men how to make war, and they came to get him. They bound him up and took him away. I thought they were going to take me too.

You have never seen anything quite as frightening to look upon as an Archangel." He lowered his voice and looked me in the eyes.

"Don't get me wrong they are not monstrous looking like the Dark Ones. Quite the contrary, they are absolutely stunning, but fierce looking, like the gigantic, unbeatable warriors that they are. They all bent down to look at me as if deciding what my fate would be. I heard a voice I shall never forget. Just the sound of it made me want to weep. It was like if thunder could make words, all it said was 'Leave the boy.' The Archangels stood up then and left taking my father with them." Zell finished the story and our dinner at about the same time. He laid our dinner on a low table in front of the fire.

"You say your race is called the Anak?"

"We are also called Nephilim or Jedi. I read one piece of research that suggested the union between the celestial angels and the human women corrupted the DNA code, and that corruption explains why the Anak were bloodthirsty giants. Whether true or not, I don't know, but it makes sense."

"Come," he said simply taking my hand and leading me from the sofa to a pillow lying beside a low table in front of a crackling fire. He sat down on a cushion on the opposite side of the table. He bowed his head and raised his hands. I probably should have too, but I didn't pray anymore which of course hurt my father. I couldn't help it. God let my mother die. I wasn't going to pray to him. Instead, I watched Zell with fascination.

"Ancient of Days, we honor you and ask your blessings to be bestowed upon us. Amen." Zell prayed simply.

He opened his eyes and looked at me. "You are my blessing," Zell stated quietly looking deep into my eyes. He reached out where my left hand laid on top of the table and covered it with his own. My breath caught in my throat, and I could not tear my eyes away from his lovely gaze. For long minutes, we sat there ignoring our dinner absorbed in simply looking at one another.

Finally, Zell broke the spell and said, "Eat so you can spend the next few hours telling me what a terrific chef I am."

After we finished what turned out to be an amazing dinner, Zell took my hand and lifted me to my feet. I have no television here, but remember I am the perfect mimic. I can sing to you. Who will it be?" he said laughing. "Elvis, Elton John, Barry Manilow, 50 Cent, who?"

"Barry Manilow, 50 Cent? Really? Can you play an instrument?"

"Yes," he answered simply.

"Well, which instrument?" I asked thinking he was playing with me.

"All of them," Zell answered matter-of-fact.

"All of them?" I echoed.

"Eternity is quite a long time. I had to do something to occupy my time when I wasn't killing the other Anak who came for me or the Dark Ones. I learned to play instruments, one at a time, until I mastered them all." He moved to a shelf on the wall opposite the fireplace and took down an instrument that resembled a guitar, but the back was rounded instead of flat. He sat down on the sofa next to me and began to play softly. It was the most beautiful melody that I had ever heard. Then he began a melody that sounded familiar. When he started to sing, I knew the song.

"Wise men say only fools rush in,
But I can't help falling in love with you
Shall I stay?
Would it be a sin?
If I can't help falling in love with you

Like a river flows surely to the sea
Darling, so it goes.
Some things are meant to be . . ."

When he finished, I was almost speechless.

"That was my mom and dad's song. My mother told me it was the song playing the first time she and dad slow danced. It was the song they danced to at their wedding too. She actually had an album collection of Elvis Presley's. Dad still has it. I'll show it to you sometime," I said my voice falling away with those last words.

"What's the matter?" Zell asked.

"I feel rotten. Really, this isn't fair to Jon. I'm with you on this beautiful island, and you just played the most romantic song ever. This is hard," I whispered my voice breaking.

"Why Annie?"

"Because."

"Because?" he whispered back taking my hand.

"Because it would be so easy to fall for you in a moment like this."

"Then fall," Zell whispered taking me in his arms. "This will be our song too."

He started to sing the song again a cappella pulling me up from the sofa and slow dancing with me in his arms. I was falling for him. I knew it, but I would not be human if I was not swept up in the romantic moment. He is singing a love song that has a special meaning to me. He is handsome, attentive, a graceful dancer, and his voice is amazing. I didn't want this moment to end, ever. When he finished the song, his hand traveled up my arm to my chin. Lifting it, he raised my face to meet his.

"I love you, Annie."

"Don't say that, please."

"Why?" He asked searching my face.

"I barely know you."

"Ok sweetheart, I've waited what seems to have been an eternity for you, but I can wait forever if that is what you desire. Come, you may choose the next song," he said guiding me back to the sofa.

He played for hours. Each tune was more intoxicating than the one before. Before long, I began to sing with him. When we ran out of songs that I knew, we began to sing silly songs laughing so hard we could barely finish them.

Between the music, my full stomach, the warmth of the fire, and listening to Zell play, my eyes began to grow heavy and my eyelids fluttered. Zell noticed immediately and stopped playing.

He helped me up and showed me into an expansive bedroom. He laid one of his large tee shirts on a monstrous bed. "I'll build a fire in here, and then I will go outside while you change," he said. Quickly, he built the fire and strode from the room and the house in a few short strides grabbing the sheath of one of his swords as he passed it.

I undressed and put on his tee shirt whose hem almost touched my knees. The hem of the arms came below my elbows. I found a brush lying on the table next to the bed and brushed my hair until it shone. I faced the huge bed, turned down the sheets and coverlet, and I actually had to climb up on it to get in bed. I propped up on the pillows watching the fire crackling across the room and pulled the covers up to my chin.

Zell walked back through the door and smiled at me. His smile warmed me as much as the fire. He strode to the fire and put on several more logs. He crossed the room to where he had left his other swords and moved them to the table next to the opposite side of the bed still holding the one he had carried outside with him in his right hand. He laid that sword at the end of the bed.

"I'm going to change," Zell told me and left the room.

Panic hit me. I turned facing the wall and worried. What was I doing here in this desolate place with a virtual stranger? Suddenly, I longed for home and my bed. Whatever happened to me, I deserved it for not demanding that he take me home.

I heard Zell laugh. "You can turn around now, Annie."

Slowly, I did as he asked. I breathed a sigh of relief when I saw Zell was dressed. Although, he was dressed only in a pair of soft silver silk trousers with a drawstring waist, I felt relieved.

He sat on top of the covers, and I was safely beneath them. I turned facing the wall again. Zell sat against pillows that were resting on a massive mahogany headboard. He bent to retrieve the sword left at the end of the bed and laid his left arm in which his hand held the sword protectively across me.

"I have a confession to make, Annie," Zell whispered sighing. This moment was incredible. The only light emanated from the crackling fire. The bed was so soft, warm, and comfortable, and Zell's lovely voice was speaking to me. I was so sleepy, and yet I didn't want this night to end.

"I knew it was your mother's favorite song. The first time I heard her play it, I knew I would sing it to you one day. Good night, love," Zell's voice was barely audible as he pressed a kiss to the top of my head.

I was in the car with my mother. She was driving and fighting off a monster at the same time. The monster looked human though his eyes were the color of blood. He bared his lips in a hiss exposing two large fangs on either side of his mouth. Mother screamed and stabbed him with a pen in one of his eyes while still driving and trying to maintain control of the car. Blood spurted all over my mother as the monster sank its razor-sharp fangs into her neck.

I cried out as our vehicle left the road. When we hit the ground again, the safety belt which the creature had cut with his claws as he tried to reach me broke in two and threw me forward through an open window. I could see a massive tree coming at me fast. A millisecond before impact something stopped me. Then I heard the same hiss I had heard before behind me. Clutching the thing that cradled me, I turned seeing the monster that attacked my mother coming for me. I saw a blade extended before me etched in a familiar looking ancient manuscript. I followed the blade to the arm that held it, then upward to that exquisite face from my dreams and now my life. Zell was in this nightmare. One wing covered my eyes as he dealt a death blow to the chest of the creature. Just before the wing covered my eyes, I saw her, my mother, there in the distance, behind the monster in the wreck of her car. My mother's lifeless body was slumped over the steering wheel covered in her blood. Her unseeing eyes looked toward me. I sobbed loudly.

"Wake up Annie. Shhh, it's only a dream." Zell held me in his arms rocking me back and forth. I could see him in the glow of the firelight. I threw my arms about his neck grasping his hair with both hands and pulled his lips to mine. I kissed him as I had never kissed a boy before. With all the passion that I possessed, I kissed him deeply. I could feel rather than see the surprise in Zell, and he hesitated momentarily before returning my kiss. Then, he returned my kiss with a passion so deep that my head swam dizzily. He held me to him as if he were afraid I might disappear if he loosened his hold. I met his passion with my own, and we were both spiraling into a crevasse of desire. The next moment, Zell tore himself from me and strode to the hearth of the fireplace. Resting his forearm on the mantel, he gazed into the fire.

"Annie don't. I'm only human, half-human that is, and the other part that is not human is evil. My father took my mother against her will. She was a good woman. He ruined her life. Back in the ancient days, a woman who conceived a child out of wedlock was stoned to death. My mother had to leave her village, her family, everything she knew until her time was passed. My aunt Miriam told everyone in the village that my mother had gone to the village of

her betrothed to be married, but we lived in the
wilderness in a tent.   When I was two, we moved
back to my mother's village. My Aunt Miriam
covered for her once again telling the people of the
village that my father was a solider and had gone off
to war. Times have changed I know, but I won't take
you outside of marriage. I was conceived when my
father forced himself on my mother. I won't be my
father's son. I'm sorry; I can't. You're too young. I
didn't bring you here to seduce you. I can't do that to
you or betray your father's trust in you. I have sworn
to protect you always. What kind of protector would I
be if I took advantage of you?" Zell hung his head
speaking into the fire, but I could see both his fists
clenched at his side in a display of willpower.

Of course, his kiss had left me a quivering mess as
before. I wanted to tell him that I was sorry. I wanted
to tell him the moment was all my fault. I don't know
what I was thinking. I wasn't thinking. I reacted to his
tenderness in a way that I never thought that I would.
I could not orally respond or apologize, so I lay my
head back on the pillow and closed my eyes.

When I opened them again, the light of morning
was filtering gently through the windows. Zell was
laying on top of the covers on his side asleep. His
arms covered me protectively. His sword was still
drawn and in his hand. Had I just dreamed the
passionate scene from last night? I didn't think so. It
was too real. I blushed just thinking about it.

Suddenly, I felt great and wanted to be up and
exploring the island. I turned in Zell's arms, and
patted him on the cheek.

"Wake up sleepy head," I spoke quietly. "I want
to go exploring."

Zell opened one eye and looked at me intently as if deciding whether I was worth opening the other eye. He smiled his wide, beautiful grin.

"Good morning, beautiful," he whispered.

"Get up silly," I said squirming out from underneath his massive arm and sword. "I want to explore this island."

Zell laughed and hopped up returning his sword to its sheath.

"Are you paranoid?" I asked. "What could possibly come after us on this island?"

With a serious scowl on his face, Zell turned to look at me. "We are not safe anywhere on this planet."

My mouth dropped open at his words.

"However, we are as safe here as we can be. Safe enough that I allowed myself to fall asleep," he added reassuringly. "How about a morning swim?"

I returned his enthusiasm for a swim, but I remembered that I didn't have a bathing suit.

"Look in the top drawer of that chest. You'll find anything you need in there. I just wanted you to wear my tee shirt last night, so when we go back home I can lay it beside me at night and smell your perfume."

"That's gross," I yelled throwing a pillow and hitting him in the chest. I was up for any challenge this day brought. Hurriedly, I dressed. Zell was waiting outside for me when I finished putting on the sleek, black, one-piece suit I found in the chest.

Zell put his sheaths around his neck and took my hand.

"Let's go." We walked in silence to the edge of the bluff.

"How do we get to the beach?" I asked peering over the edge of the cliff.

Without a word, he released my hand and stepped back a few feet. Zell closed his eyes and concentrated. What I saw next was incredible. Huge white wings tipped in silver and black stretched up towards the heavens and spread elegantly open. There were four of them. The top wings on each side stretched toward the heavens, while the lower wings wrapped around his body like caressing arms. What a resplendent sight he made just standing there! He opened his eyes and ran toward me scooping me up in his arms as he leaped from the cliff. Screaming in fear, I clutched him tightly. His top wings spread above us like a parachute, and his bottom wings and arms held me gently. We floated down to a small sandy beach at the base of the cliff. Even after we landed, I could not force my fingers to release their death grip from around his neck.

"That was amazing! Can we do it again?" I cried.

Zell threw his head back and laughed. "I have been reduced to an amusement park ride." He gathered me in his arms and shot like a rocket into the heavens. When the island was just a dot in the water, he hovered hugging me to him. "Ready?" he asked.

I had barely caught my breath from our vertical climb, yet I nodded my head yes. He suddenly dropped like a speeding elevator. The ground was coming at us fast when his top wings popped out like a parachute, and we floated down to the beach.

"That was so much fun," I laughed when he released me and ran toward the water. I stopped at the edge of the water and the smile faded from my lips. "What about sharks?"

"I am the predator here. No sharks will dare come near us. There is a family of dolphins that swim around here though. They may swim with us." As if on cue, three large and two small dolphins poked their heads out of the water chattering in their dolphin language as if inviting us for a swim.

6. THE COOKOUT

ZELL AND I LAY ON THE BEACH DRYING in the mid-day sun. All the swimming made me famished. I was exhausted but happy. The dolphins enjoyed our company and played in the water with us for hours. I held on to their dorsal fins, and they pulled me gliding effortlessly through the water. Zell was always protectively at my side. I turned over on my stomach in order to see Zell and talk to him.

"I have to go back today."

"I know," Zell answered not looking at me. "I wish you didn't."

"Me too," I replied quietly. "I've promised everyone that I am going to the cookout tonight at Lauren's beach house. You know how I am with promises."

"Yes, I know." Silence stretched for several minutes then Zell said, "Do you really wish that you could stay here? If you do, please stay. It is dangerous for you to go to the party Annie."

"Nevertheless, I'm going," I stated flatly.

"Correction, we're going," Zell insisted.

"But Jon will be there."

"Who?"

"You know perfectly well who."

"Isn't it about time you broke up with that guy?"

"Why should I?"

"You have me now. You don't need him anymore."

"I never did need him, but he's my friend."

Zell turned on his side and looked into my eyes.

"Do you remember what happened on Tuesday night, Annie?"

"You mean the night before you enrolled in school here?"

"Yes."

"Not really. I remember staying after practice with Kate to shoot free throws. The next thing I remember is waking up late the following morning."

"You were almost attacked, Annie. A creature tracked you to the parking lot. If I had not been there, . . ."

"Not this Dark One Myth again," I groaned.

"Am I a myth? Do I not exist?" Zell answered never raising his voice.

"Of course, you do, but just like you said you're the only one of your kind."

"Yes, my kind, but a Dark One is not my kind."

"I think you're only looking for a reason to hang out with me, Zell and for a reason for me to dump Jon. You have yourself believing in this whole boogie man thing. You believe you need to protect me to justify you being with me," I threw back at him.

"What about the dreams, Annie?"

"I've always had bad dreams ever since my mother died."

"What killed her Annie?" Zell moved within inches of my face.

"A car crash killed her," I yelled back at him.

"What really killed her Annie?" Zell kept pushing me for an answer.

"Take me home, Zell. I want to go home," my voice began to quiver.

"You know it's all true Annie. Your nightmares are not dreams. They are memories," Zell said forcefully yet calmly.

"That's not true," I spat back at him.

Zell stood up then towering above me. He snapped his wings up like a Geisha Girl snaps out her fan. The wings popped into place. Zell pulled me to him covering me to protect me from the wind and gave a great push. We soared upward so fast that the movement took my breath and made me a bit nauseated, but it was more thrilling than anything I had ever experienced. We landed outside the cottage door, and Zell ordered me inside to change. He followed closely behind me grabbing his clothes and then stalking back out the door. When I emerged from the cottage, he was dressed and waiting on me. He held his arms out, and I moved into them. It seemed to only be minutes later, and we were standing beside my car.

"Come in while I change into fresh clothes. Then, I will take you home."

I followed him into the mansion through a massive wooden door that reminded me of the door on the island cottage only more ornate. Suddenly, I stopped in front of the door. The same ancient writing that I had seen etched on a sword in my nightmares was engraved into Zell's front door. Gently, I traced the letters with my fingers.

"What is this writing?" I asked turning to Zell.

"It is Aramaic,"

"What does it say?"

"It is a quote from the Bible."

"What is the quote?" I asked softly.

"Proverbs 18:10. 'The name of the LORD is a strong tower: the righteous runneth into it, and is safe.'"

I smiled at his words running my fingertips over the writing.

"Lovely," I whispered, and then turned as if drawn by the beauty of his home. It took my breath away. Someone had a fire burning in a massive marble fireplace, and beautiful music drifted throughout the house. The lamps were on giving the room a soft glow. The firelight flickered off warm, wooden vaulted ceilings. There were only windows on two sides of the house. The back and left side butted up against a stone bluff. I thought it very strange. There was plenty of room to build in front of the house. It wasn't necessary for anyone to build into the bluff. It reminded me of a fortress. Then it hit me. It was a fortress! Zell built the house into the stone face of the bluff to prevent anyone from coming in on those sides. He only had to defend himself on two sides.

I wandered around the immaculate living and dining rooms picking up artifacts that looked to be thousands of years old. One was a stone tablet sitting on a sofa table on an ornate easel. The writing on the tablet was the same as the writing engraved on the door. About that time, Zell entered the room in a pair of off-white jeans, leather sandals, and a loose-fitting yellow, silk shirt. The sun from our swim gave his skin and hair a beautiful glow. His silver eyes sparkled against the bronze of his skin. He was breathtaking. Any girl in her right mind would love to have him as her own. Why was I holding on to Jon when this magnificent creature was clearly interested in me? I wanted to run to him and throw myself in his arms, but I resisted the impulse and instead asked him to drive me home.

"Certainly," Zell replied coolly.

In the car on the ride to my house, Zell asked what time he should pick me up for the cookout at Lauren's lake house.

"I'm going with Jon. I have already promised him," I stated hesitantly.

"Annie, that's not wise," Zell looked and sounded very concerned.

"Nonsense," I retorted sharply.

"Very well," Zell answered as if he knew arguing with me would not get him anywhere. "But know this, I will not be far from you if you need me or desire to change your date for the evening." Zell turned and gazed at me warmly. The smile that slowly spread across his face was dazzling. His smile made me wish that he *was* my date for the evening.

"About last night, everything after dinner is kind of fuzzy, but if I was out of line, I apologize. I think I dreamed of the death of my mother, and when I awoke, all of those pent-up emotions seemed to take over. Your kiss is responsible for the fuzziness of my memory, I guess. I can only remember bits and pieces, but I'm sorry. I'm don't regret that I kissed you. I only regret is that it got out of hand. It was totally my fault not yours.

Zell walked me to the door and without touching me he whispered, "No worries. Until later."

Zell drove me from school in my car, and that is
the car in which he now drove me home. "How are
you getting home?" I asked perplexed.

"Annie, really?" Zell laughed taking off his shirt,
popping out his wings, and taking off like a rocket.

"Zell, the neighbors . . ." I yelled into the air, but
he was gone.

A couple of hours later, Jon rang the doorbell. Dr.
Hayes, my father, answered the door. Dad looked
every bit the intellectual that he was. His short crew
cut hair stuck out in all directions. Smoky blue eyes
that I inherited from him were framed in round, horn-
rimmed spectacles. Speaking softly, he greeted Jon at
the door.

"Good evening, Jon."

"Good evening, Dr. Hayes," Jon answered
absently looking around the room for me.

"Annie will be right down. Won't you have a
seat?" my father invited.

As if on cue, I swept into the room and kissed my
father on the cheek.

"Good night, Dad. I won't be late."

"Have a good time sweetheart, and please be
careful," Dad admonished. His daughter seemed to
have a knack for finding adventure and that fact
worried him immensely.

I thought if he only knew the unbelievable events
of the last few days, he would have a stroke.

Jon opened the door for me, and we stepped out
into the night air.

"You look amazing," Jon told me as we walked to
his Dodge truck. At the truck, he tried to kiss me
before I climbed in, but I deftly avoided his kiss and
hopped into the passenger side of the truck.

"Thanks, you look nice too."

Jon hesitated for a moment swinging the passenger door back and forth with his right hand while his left arm was propped up on the roof of his truck. He opened his mouth and then closed it. I knew he was angry because I avoided his kiss. He decided against saying anything, and he slammed the door and stalked around to the driver's side.

My thoughts, however, were on Zell. Would he wear what he had on when he dropped me off this afternoon? I hoped so. It was the perfect attire for a lake house cookout. Thinking about what Zell had worn this afternoon, I had also dressed in an off-white jean skirt, a yellow sleeveless sweater, and silver sandals. My hair was clean and shiny, pulled back with a thin silver headband that showed off the tan my face had received at the island earlier that day. It was still too early in the season at the lake to have a tan. I worried that Zell and I would stick out like sore thumbs with the tan we both had received today at the beach on his island in the middle of the ocean hundreds of miles south from here. It was still unbelievable, and I could not get my mind off Zell and the events of the last few days. I tried to think of something to say to Jon, but I was overwhelmed by the prospect that there may be dark creatures who hunt me, and a lone Zell to protect me.

Why *was* I here with Jon? I could not keep my thoughts from wandering to Zell. I had only known him for a few days, but I felt as though there were a bond between us that was timeless. I turned my head in the truck to look at Jon and caught him staring at me strangely. The look in his eyes gave me the oddest sensation.

"What are you thinking about?"

"You," he replied. "You seem different somehow."

"Really, how so?"

"I don't know, but it's as if your thoughts are miles away, not here with me."

I laughed, "That's silly." However, I turned away from him to look out the window into the night afraid that he would see on my face that things were indeed different, inescapably so. Somewhere Zell was out there. Was he close by? He said that he would not be far away if I needed him or wanted to change my date for the evening. I was beginning to want that. I wanted Zell to be my date. I was beginning to want Zell to be my life.

"Stop it!" I yelled.

"What?" Jon yelled back slamming on the brakes. In confusion, he turned to look at me. "What was that all about?"

"I'm sorry. I wasn't talking to you. I was talking to myself. I was thinking of something else," I replied embarrassed.

"You about gave me a heart attack. I thought I was about to have a wreck!" Jon yelled at me, then revved the engine, popped the clutch with a violent jerk, and began to drive again.

What an idiot I am! I was thinking about Zell while I'm with Jon, and then almost vocalized that fact. Dumb. Dumb. Dumb. I thought I heard laughter and turned to look out the back window of the truck. He was out there laughing at me. I could feel him near. My embarrassment turned to anger quickly. I slid across the seat next to Jon and laid my head against his arm as he drove. I smiled smugly. Take that Zell!

Jon turned to look at me next to him with a puzzled look on his face.

"What is up with you tonight, Annie? First, you're yelling at me to stop, and all I am doing is driving. Then you slide across the seat and snuggle up against me. Something that you never do. You have avoided my every touch for days. What gives?" Jon asked.

"I've just missed you?" I guessed scrambling for an excuse.

"Excuse me if I don't quite swallow that. Who is this new guy who claims to be your boyfriend?" Jon demanded.

"His name is Zell Starr."

"Yeah, yeah, I know that. He introduced himself in class remember?"

"Oh yeah," I said sheepishly.

"Who is *he*?" Jon demanded louder this time emphasizing the *he*.

"Just a friend," I answered innocently.

"Who claims to be your boyfriend," Jon returned jealously.

"He is just exaggerating. We are only friends, and I have told him that," I said turning red with embarrassment as I thought about last night and how I had kissed him when he woke me from my nightmare, or was it the nightmare? My life and my nightmares were becoming so entangled that I could not tell the difference.

"He looks like he believes you two are a couple."

"We are definitely not a couple."

"I'll take care of him," Jon ground out smugly. "If he shows up tonight, I'm going to tell him to stay away from you. If that doesn't give him the message, these will," he boasted holding up both fists.

"You will not, Jonathan Howard. He is my friend too." I panicked at the thought of Jon even trying to 'take care of' Zell. Zell would kill him. I didn't even think it would be much of a fight. "Please Jonny, promise me you won't say anything to him."

"No, I won't promise," Jon insisted.

"Jon, if you say anything to Zell, I promise that I will never, and I mean never, speak to you or see you again," I threatened.

"You like this guy, don't you," Jon asked turning to look at me.

"Watch the road, Jon," I demanded. "It's just that Zell is my friend too. I don't want to lose either of you."

"You can't have us both, Annie. You have to choose," Jon gave me an ultimatum.

"That's not fair!"

"Maybe not, but that's how it is. Decide Annie. It's the overgrown immigrant or me."

"O.K.," I said gritting my teeth. "I choose . . . I choose neither of you." Jon stopped in front of Lauren's lake house, and I jumped from the truck and slammed the door. The house was lit up welcoming and inviting, but I ducked around the side of the house heading for the sound of laughter coming from the back. I stopped suddenly. I felt like I did the night of . . . the night of . . . The night of what? This was getting infuriating. Why couldn't I remember? Some memory was there just out of my reach. Maybe it was so terrifying that my mind would not let me remember. Nevertheless, something was in the woods to my right. I could feel it watching me. I picked up speed and ran toward the spotlights in the backyard. As I turned the corner of the house, I turned and watched the woods for the unknown predator that I was sure lurked there.

Thud. I felt like I hit a brick wall. Looking up, I saw Zell staring down at me.

"Watch where you are going! You stay away from me too!" I yelled at him and instantly felt bad for speaking to him that way. I was too rattled to be with him right now though, and I stepped around him to find Lauren and Kate. I saw Kate in the gazebo on the other side of the pool and hurried to her.

"Annie, what's wrong? You look like you've seen a ghost," said Kate worriedly.

"Nah, just an Anak," I replied.

"A what?" asked Kate.

I laughed, "Nothing Kate. Jon and I just had a fight that's all."

"What about?"

"What else? My new boyfriend, Zell, which traveled here from Europe to be with me."

"Yeah, I'm mad about that, Annie. You never told me that you met someone in Europe."

"I didn't tell you because I didn't meet him in Europe," I said my voice low and quivering.

"I'm lost," Kate replied.

"I never met Zell until Wednesday morning in the school office. I don't know what's going on," I grabbed the water Kate was drinking and drank from the bottle.

"I'm still confused. Why would anyone as gorgeous as Zell lie about knowing you?"

"He says he is here to protect me," I whispered furtively looking about.

"Protect you from what?"

"The Dark Ones, can you believe that?"

"What's a Dark One?" Kate asked puzzled.

"Vampires, werewolves, demons, Fallen Angels, some incognito, of course, et cetera," I whispered shaking my head and lowering my voice even further searching every shadow for a monster.

Kate howled with laughter then suddenly stopped as the events of the evening at the gym a few days ago came vividly back into focus.

"You're scaring me, Annie," Kate whispered back.

"Huh, you're scared. I'm beginning to believe him. Weird things have been happening in the last few days. I think something may be after me."

"Annie, you're being ridiculous," Kate scolded.

"Maybe, maybe not. I'm not sure of anything right now. All I know is that something strange is going on."

"Are you sure Zell is who he says he is? Do you think he might be behind all this?" Kate asked.

"I'm pretty sure he is different, really different," I replied drinking the last of the water.

"Different? You're right about that. He is the most handsome person I've ever seen. If you don't want him, can I have him?" Kate gushed.

"Yeah, he's a real angel alright." I growled pacing back and forth.

Someone brought out a guitar, and Rylee asked Zell to play. A crowd gathered around him. Savanna, Maddison, Whitney, the lovely LeeAnn, Rylee, Lauren, Natalie, Kenzley, Holly, in fact, most of the girls at the party sat at his feet. Zell leaned against a low stone wall and began strumming the guitar. Most guys stood at the fringes of the crowd scowling. All their girlfriends were at Zell's feet totally focused on him. Zell began to play beautifully. Someone yelled out a song and instantly Zell changed the tune to the requested song. Time and again, he did this. It was amazing. He never left out a note or broke the rhythm of the song. Even the guys began to be mesmerized by his ability.

Zell stopped for a moment and looked at me. Then he began to sing a beautiful love song, never once taking his eyes from my face. I could feel the strong emotions from last night wash over me. I've never lost a struggle once I set my mind to something, but this was one battle that I was losing fast. The beautiful song he sang, "My Destiny" seemed as though it had been written for us.

"From now until eternity,
You were always meant to be,
My destiny"

Zell sang through the song a couple of times never taking his eyes off me. He finished and handed the guitar back to Lauren. His female audience stood to their feet applauding and squealing like little school girls. Zell still focused on me, stood up, and started in my direction. Savanna grabbed his arm and tried to get him to stay with her. Ever the gentleman, Zell leaned over and whispered something in her ear removing her hand from his arm as he did so. He headed for me again. Just as he rounded the pool, Jon popped up as if from thin air.

"Annie, I'm sorry," Jon began. It was all I could do to tear my eyes from Zell and attempt to focus on Jon.

"Oh, the drama," Kate said giggling. "Annie, your love life is actually getting interesting. Way to go girl."

Jon threw a deadly look in Kate's direction and grabbed my hand dragging me from the gazebo.

"Let's go somewhere, so we can speak in private," Jon huffed still glaring at Kate.

"No, Jon, I can't." I resisted, but Jonny pulled me along anyway. Behind him, I could see the crowd catch up to Zell, and he paused staring at us grimacing when he saw Jon grab my hand. Jon dragged me down toward the shore of the lake.

Lauren's dad had made a beach out of their property that ran along the lake. He had truckloads of sand brought in and dredged out the bottom of the lake near the shoreline to create a smooth and safe beach. Her dad, Chuck, was one of the big wigs at Turner Broadcasting. He was very wealthy, and Lauren had him wrapped around her finger. What Lauren wanted; Lauren got. There was a dock with a diving board, a speedboat, a half-dozen Sea Doos, little paddlewheel boats, and canoes all housed under a covered dock that ran a couple of hundred feet in an L shape into the lake. Even so, I didn't think even Chuck's wealth could equal Zell's.

Torches were lit all along the shore and gas lamps lit the docks. Big comfortable chairs for lounging or sunbathing were scattered over the beach, and Jon pulled me toward a couple of them. I sat down on one of the overstuffed chairs, and Jon sat opposite me.

"Annie, I'm sorry. I don't want to break up with you," he began.

"We don't go together. We're just friends," I huffed as I interrupted him.

"I want to change that Annie. I want you to be my girl," Jon begged pulling off his senior ring and holding it out for me to take. I suddenly shivered uncontrollably. Goose bumps stood at full attention on my arms and neck. Jon noticed me shivering.

"I'll run to the truck and get your jacket," Jon said and jumped up running toward the house before I could tell him not to bother.

Back at the pool, Zell watched as Jon pulled me toward the beach. Anger burned within him, but before he could react, a hand once again grabbed his arm and locked around it. It was LeeAnn. Lee Ann was beautiful. The moonlight and the soft lights of the backyard area softened her features making her even more attractive.

"Stay with me," LeeAnn cooed.

"LeeAnn, you are incredibly lovely, but my heart is somewhere else," Zell stated flatly. "Please release me. I have to go."

"I can make you happy, Zell," Lee Ann suggestively offered as Zell placed his hand over hers.

"You will make someone very happy, but I'm not the one. Annie makes me happy," Zell replied as he once again lifted her fingers from his arm.

"But Annie's taken," LeeAnn sulked.

The pain of her words showed on his face. Zell felt as if the breath was knocked out of him. He turned without a reply and walked toward the beach unbuttoning his shirt as he walked.

I shivered again, and this time every hair on my body stood up on end. I looked to where the dark forms of trees met the sand and saw a figure separate from the trees. Immobilized with fear, I couldn't scream or cry out. The figure seemed to glide quickly toward me. I tried to run toward the house, but I could not move. I tried to scream, but nothing came out. I tried again to move, but it was as though I was frozen in time. My voice would not work. My legs and feet felt as though they weighed a ton. As the dark figure neared, I could see that its body was shaped like a man's, but its eyes were the eyes of a creature, red as blood. The figure was within striking distance of me when it slowed.

"Where is your savior, now?" the thing hissed at me. As he did, I could see a gleaming set of teeth reflecting in the light of the torches, two, three-inch fangs, hung menacingly from an otherwise impeccable set of teeth. The creature reached for me with a hand who's blue, dead looking nails were like sharpened knives.

I shrank from him. Instantly, he was within inches of my face. He was incredible looking. Handsome, in a hellish kind of way, his features were every bit as attractive as Zell's except his eyes were that of the dead, cold and unseeing. Instead of Zell's beautiful silver-colored eyes, this creature's eyes were red and dilated.

Everything in me said to run. Run for my life. I honestly tried, but I could not move. The creature bared his lips and opened his mouth. He grabbed the neck of my sweater and ripped it back exposing the flesh of my neck. Jumping backward, I fell over one of the beach chairs.

"Now," he growled, "I'm going to rip your throat out." Grabbing me by the sweater, he jerked me up, and bent his head. He was centimeters from sinking his razor-sharp teeth and fangs into my neck when suddenly his head snapped back with a grinding crunch.

"Get off her, bloodsucker."

His body was thrown backwards a hundred feet across the beach hitting the side of the dock. I could hear the sound of breaking bones as he hit. I forgot everything when I looked into the face of my hero. Standing tall and magnificent in the moonlight, stood Zell. He was still impeccably dressed in his off-white jeans and sandals. Though bare-chested, his silver sheaths that held his swords laid against his massive chest as if they were a part of him. He reached to take my hand.

Crying out his name, I jumped into his arms instead.

"Have you been bitten?" Zell asked pushing my hair back to inspect my neck.

"I don't think so."

At that second, we both heard the sound of breaking bones again and turned to look. The vampire's body snapped back into place from its broken form. Waist-deep in lake water, it stood upright. The sound of bones pop, pop, popping back into place filled the silence and drifted toward us as the vampire's head and neck jerked back upright to sit once again upon his shoulders. An arm that was hanging at a grotesque angle snapped around 180 degrees.

Zell turned looking at me.

"Run! Run back to the lights and the house," Zell ordered and then turned facing the dark creature. He began to change and grow. He was becoming as fearsome as he was beautiful. His jeans ripped open as his muscular form tore through.

I took a couple of steps in the direction of the house and stopped. I could not make myself leave Zell. If he died, I didn't want to live either. I had known him only a few days, but he had become part of me. I'm not sure when it had happened, but I was sure that I would never get over it if I lost him now.

"Are you crazy?" I asked myself. "You've only known this guy a few days." However, even as those thoughts formed on my lips, I knew that it was not the truth. I could feel memories flooding into me tumbling one over another into my brain as I saw him shape-shift into his Anak transformation. I knew this was not the first time Zell had saved me, and I would not leave him.

I looked back toward the dock and saw the vampire leap into the air in Zell's direction. I heard the whispering metallic sounds of swords being withdrawn from their sheaths. Zell faced the vampire with swords drawn and in each hand.

The vampire landed within a few feet of Zell.

"I'll finish you. Then, I'll drain your girlfriend," the Dark One snarled teeth glittering like jewels in the moonlight.

"I don't think you will do either," Zell countered.

The vampire snarled moving to Zell's right. Zell countered his actions by moving with him, keeping himself between the vampire and me.

The vamp leaped for me. Zell met him about fifteen feet straight up in the air. Their bodies collided making a thunderous noise. The ground trembled beneath my feet causing me to lose my balance. The lights from the house and boat docks flickered, and then the lights went out. The vampire sank its teeth into Zell's arm. Zell grabbed him by the hair of his head and threw him to the ground. Instantly, he followed him and drove the swords into the body of the vampire. The vampire was quick, and instead of driving the swords through the heart of the creature as he intended, they pierced his shoulder.

The beast screeched an inhuman howl that caused every dog within two miles to start barking. The vampire rose stiffly as if from a coffin, the swords still buried in his shoulder. Zell grabbed the hilt of each sword, and placed his foot against the belly of the creature. He pushed the creature with his foot while simultaneously pulling the swords from the shoulder of the vamp. The vampire screeched an inhuman sound again flinging itself in my direction sand flying up in a spray from behind him as he moved. Zell met him once more tackling him, as though he were a football opponent causing another horrendous noise, which sounded like a clap of thunder. I could hear squeals from the pool area near the house as my friends sought cover thinking it was about to rain. Both hit the sand and rolled toward the water. When they stopped rolling, the creature was on top, and Zell was holding him off with his swords.

I did not think about what I did next. I grabbed one of the flaming torches and yanked it from the sand. I ran toward where the vampire had Zell pinned to the ground and drove the pointed bottom of the wooden, burning torch into the back of the creature.

The vampire threw its head back and let out an inhuman howl that made my blood run cold. Zell threw the creature from him and jumped to his feet. He walked to where the creature had landed and drove both swords into the heart of the creature. He pulled his flaming sword from his back sheath and amputated the vampire's legs. They instantly caught fire and began to burn. Then, he cut the arms and watched as they burst into flames. Next, he separated the head from the creature. It too began to burn from the flame of the sword while the vampire's head, though separated from its body, still hissed and hurled profanities at him. Next, he withdrew his swords one by one and returned them to their sheaths. Finally, he thrust the flaming sword into the gaping holes left by his swords, and what was left of the torso of the vampire burst into flames.

I ran to Zell jumping into his arms, wrapping my legs around his waist, and burying my head into his shoulder.

"Are you hurt," I asked rubbing my fingers over the wound on his arm.

"No," Zell replied looking at the blood running down his arm, "Dark Ones don't affect me the way they do humans. It's just a bite. Be careful the blood doesn't get on you. It is full of bacteria and deadly to humans."

"Would I turn into one of those if it bit me?"

"No, but you would most likely die." Zell wiped the blood from his arm with a towel someone had left draped over a chair on the beach.

"I need to shift before someone comes, and I need to find my shirt," he whispered. Zell held the towel in place stemming the flow of blood while I looked for his shirt. He paused and began to shift back into his human form from that of the Anak. He slowly shrunk by several feet as the alabaster glow faded from his body, and color crawled back into his skin. I found his shirt lying on a shrub and ran back to him with it. Zell smiled sweetly at me.

"Thank you," he said simply.

I helped him slip it on over the sheaths that were still in place. Zell pulled back the towel making sure the wound had stopped bleeding. He threw the bloody towel on the vamp bonfire.

"Does it hurt much?"

"Just stings a bit," he replied as he buttoned his shirt. As if on cue, as soon as the last button was buttoned, Jon stepped onto the beach. He was in the act of handing me my jacket when he saw my sweater half ripped from my body and stopped in mid-air. I plucked the jacket from him. I quickly pulled it on and zipped it up over my torn sweater.

"Did *he* do this to you?" Jon growled.

"No, *he* didn't. Don't be a jackass Jon," I said coldly. I fell over one of the beach chairs. Zell heard me cry out and helped me. I guess my sweater caught on a nail or something."

I couldn't tell Jon it was a vampire's nail that had ripped my shirt, or the whole truth about what had just happened.

"What's that stench," Jon asked covering his nose.

"Someone set a bag of garbage on fire down by the water; I think," Zell explained.

"That is an awful smell," Jon said gagging.

"Zell is taking me home since I ripped my sweater," I calmly told Jonny.

"No, I can take you home," Jon replied still looking a somewhat greenish color. Jonny's weak stomach decided the issue for us as he began to retch on the sand forgetting about Zell and me.

I turned and took Zell's hand. We walked toward the house leaving a clueless Jon alone on the beach with the burning corpse of the vampire.

7. ZELL MEETS DAD

I FELT DISAPPOINTED WHEN ZELL LEFT ME on the doorstep at home with only a peck on the cheek. I don't know what I expected, but after saving him from the bloodsucker, I thought there would be more. I wanted more. I wanted to tell him that I was beginning to believe his outrageous story. I wanted to tell him how I was beginning to feel about him, but I didn't have the courage.

I say that I killed the vampire, but I know that Zell would have managed without my help. Yet, I did thrust a wooden pole through that vamp's black heart. That brought up another whole dilemma. I actually killed something. I know it wasn't human, and it was certainly intent on killing me. Still, I felt like I had committed a sin or something. Technically, I guess Zell ended the creature with his flame thrower, but even so, I was still an accessory to murder. If you murder a killer though, is it still murder? It was surely self-defense. That thing was getting ready to rip my throat out.

[129]

How was all this possible? The events of the night brought back jumbled memories of the monster in the school parking lot, and I knew I owed Zell my life at least twice. Maybe, there were more memories just lying there waiting to surface. Maybe, Zell saved me from sure death many times. At that moment, I decided to allow Zell into my life. When I realized that he really was there to protect me, not harm me, I knew I needed him. I knew, too, that more than just needing him, I wanted him to be with me.

I could not sleep. Every time I drifted off, nightmares would begin about vampires, giant werewolves, and silent dark angels all waiting for a chance to kill me. In my dreams, I was running from them screaming out Zell's name, but he didn't come. There were other things in the darkness. Things that were even worse, more terrifying, more evil than anything I could possibly imagine. I was in a dark, cold forest running from them, and I couldn't find Zell. They were behind me. I fell to my knees, and blood poured from a gash. They must have honed in on the smell of my blood because suddenly they were there all around me, dozens of them. Each creature more terrifying than the last. They were coming for me, closing in on me. They wanted my blood. I screamed for Zell once more, and there he was. He gathered me in his arms stroking my hair damp with perspiration.

"Shh, sweetheart, I'm here. Don't cry. I'm here. You're safe," Zell whispered in my ear.

He kissed my cheek. Then he kissed my forehead and let his lips travel down to my eyelids. Gently, he kissed each eyelid before kissing each tear on my face. Hungrily, his lips sought mine. He kissed me deeply for a long minute. I realized that he was not part of the dream, but he was here in my bedroom, sitting on my bed, calming me down with his kiss.

Like before, the mere touch of his lips on mine made me go limp. He stopped then and gently lowered me back on my pillow. Tenderly, he lifted locks of hair damp with tears and perspiration from my face. His fingers lingered on my lips. Then he rose, moved to the end of my bed, and watched as I drifted off in a deep sleep.

I overslept the next morning. It was Sunday, and Dad had knocked on my door expecting me to be up and ready for church. As a preacher's kid, I was usually dreading the never-ending Sunday; however, today I wanted to go as penance for my murder the night before. Sleepily, I rolled over and opened one eye. I remembered Zell had been here last night, and I looked around the room for him. He was gone. Disappointed, I dragged myself from the bed and washed my face in cold water. I went to find my dad.

I found him sitting in his chair by the fireplace reading.

"What are you reading?" I asked leaning over to kiss him on top of his balding head.

"*DNA Interaction Protocols,*" Dad answered smiling.

"Ugh! My dad, the ultimate nerd. Can't you ever read anything interesting?" I teased.

"But Annie, this book is very interesting. Should I take offense with the nerd comment?"

"No Dad. Everyone's dad reads about DNA interactions in their free time," I groaned and threw myself on the couch picking up the remote.

"Do you want me to make breakfast Dad?" I asked.

"No, I fixed some eggs and toast hours ago when I first got up. I left some for you in the microwave. You need to get dressed. We leave for church in thirty minutes."

My dad was a strange mix. Not only did he have a PhD in religion, but he had a Doctorate in biochemistry also.

I lay back against the cushions of the couch procrastinating about getting dressed when the doorbell rang.

Dad gently closed his book and went to answer the door.

"May I help you?" I heard my dad say politely.

"Good morning, sir." I knew the voice at once and jumped up running my fingers through the mess that was my hair. "My name is Zell Starr. I'm a friend of Annie's." I ran past my dad and Zell at the door headed for my bathroom. Zell's eyes followed me obviously amused. I caught a glimpse of the smirk on his face as I passed them.

I tore off my clothes and hopped in the shower. Before I could rinse out the lather in my hair, I heard a knock at the bathroom door.

"Annie dear, a young man named Zell is here to see you," my dad said through the door.

"I'm in the shower Dad," I yelled over the water.

"Yes, dear, I can hear that, but the young man is waiting in the living room."

"He can just wait then if he wants to see me," I yelled again over the water.

"I'll tell him," Dad mumbled. I knew he was totally confused. The only boy that who been to my house in two years was Jon. And Zell . . . well, Zell was unlike any boy I had ever seen or known. It was like Johnny Depp or Brad Pitt walking in unannounced through my front door. There was no one else like him. I'm sure my dad was wondering what in the world Zell saw in me. No, knowing my dad, he's sitting there thinking that no one will ever be good enough for me—not even this perfect young man.

I finished my shower, wrapped a towel around my head, and another around my torso. In my closet, I couldn't find anything to wear. I didn't see what Zell was wearing, but I knew it would be perfect. I chose a pale pink dress and cashmere sweater in a similar shade of pale pink. I found a pale pink pair of shoes with a three-inch padded heel to match my dress. It was nice being able to wear high heels and your date still towered over you.

"Annie, I have to leave for church. Zell has offered to drive you when you're ready. He is a friend of yours, correct?"

"Yeah, we've met," I answered sarcastically. Of course, my dad didn't understand the sarcasm, but I'm sure Zell could hear me.

I picked up the hair dryer again and resumed blowing my hair dry. For some reason, I didn't want Zell to think I was anxious to see him. He could wait. I heard the garage door open and close. I guess Dad was gone. Then, there was a soft knock at my door.

"May I come in," I heard Zell say softly.

"I guess you can. If I say no, you'll just come in anyway, so come on in."

Zell opened my door and stepped in just barely clearing the top of the door frame. My heart felt as though it would flip right up and out of my mouth. I knew how gorgeous Zell was, but it seemed as if every time I saw him, I was reamazed. He stood there in a pair of black trousers, a stiffly starched white button-down shirt and a black tie. He had on a pair of black leather shoes that looked obscenely expensive. His long, golden hair was slicked back and pulled into a small ponytail at the nape of his neck with a silver cord, real silver, I was sure. The white of his shirt set off his eyes and deep tanned complexion. He surely was a dream. No one could be this incredibly handsome.

"Are you ready, sweetheart?" Zell asked.

"Stop calling me that! I am not your sweetheart." I answered rudely.

"Well, do you want to be?" he replied with a wide smile ignoring my ill temper.

"Geez," I muttered. "I guess you're used to all the girls just falling at your feet worshiping you. Sorry, I'm not that girl. Besides don't you ever get mad? I insult you. I am rude to you. I'm mean to you, and you just smile and say something sweet. Good grief!" I said turning looking at him and rolling my eyes. Even as I said it, I knew I wasn't being honest. I could be that drooling girl in a heartbeat. Now, I'm a dishonest murderer all because of Zell, but I would still love to be his girl. I would fall at his feet too, drooling, but I did still have a shred of self-respect left. I resisted the temptation to drool. "By the way, I can drive myself."

"No, I promised your father. I, too, keep my promises."

"Oh, Ok, I'm ready then," I growled.

Zell got me to church in record time. If I didn't trust him completely, I would have been terrified, instead of just semi-terrified, of the speed with which we traveled. As we pulled in the parking lot, I let out a long sigh.

"That was the most terrifying ride that I have ever had to church or anywhere else on this planet," I spouted off pushing open the door and climbing out. When I stood and turned to tell him good-bye, Zell was already out of the car putting on a suit jacket that had been hanging in the back seat.

"Oh, no you don't. You're not coming in with me," I said even more terrified than I was on the ride over here.

"Of course I am. Your dad invited me," Zell remarked very innocently.

"You show up at my door on Sunday morning in a suit, and then talk my dad into letting you drive me to church. Of course, he invited you. You had this planned all along," I was incredulous.

"I have to be with you to protect you," Zell said innocently shrugging his shoulders.

"Nothing is going to attack me at church, Zell. I did fine until five days ago when you showed up."

"Truly? Did you really, Annie? Or, do you just think you were fine, never knowing that I had your back?" Zell asked smugly.

"You're impossible," I yelled slamming the door of his car. "Sorry." I said apologetically rubbing the car door. I *was* sorry that I had slammed the door of his exquisite car. Zell was instantly next to me. He took my arm and placed it through his, resting my hand on his forearm, and then covering it with his own hand.

"Apology accepted. It's just a car, and . . . I'm very possible," he laughingly whispered in my ear pulling me toward the door.

The pianist was already playing when we entered the back of the sanctuary. I always sat on the first pew

[135]

just to the left of the podium where my father preached, so other members of the congregation never sat there leaving that spot for me. I could hear people turn watching us pass and the whispers which rippled behind us like a wave. Zell's hand was still over mine holding it in place on his arm. I tried to slide it out from under his as we walked, but Zell applied even more pressure holding it there. He looked at me and gave me a very wicked grin. We were, unknown to the congregation, having a tug of war with my hand very subtly. When we reached my seat, I gave up the fight. Zell never released me, but he moved into position to sit in my spot on the end pulling me down next to him. My father was watching this show Zell and I were putting on with great interest. I know because I saw the corners of his mouth begin to turn up in a smile and sent him a cold glare. Dad coughed and covered his mouth.

My hand was numb by the time the service was over. Zell never took his eyes off my father or his hand from around my tightly clenched fist. He was locked in, and I could tell he was listening to every word. As for myself, I had no idea what his sermon was about. I had years of practice of drowning sermons out with my thoughts. My mind was swimming with thoughts: thoughts of killing the vampire last night swirled around in my head, Zell's arrogance at practically inviting himself to my father's church, and the domineering way he escorted me into the sanctuary locked on his arm in front of the whole congregation. I had known most of these people my entire life, and then he had the nerve to escort me down the aisle and sit in my place on the pew. Zell seems to know everything about me, so I am sure he knows that was my place where he chose to sit. I pouted. Zell listened intently to every word that came out of my father's mouth. I was so angry with Zell that I heard nothing. I had been absorbed in plotting my revenge on Zell, and I did not notice when the service ended. My father walked down the aisle to the front doors dismissing the service and waiting to shake hands with and speak to everyone as they left. Being in the first row, Zell and I were the last to approach my father, my hand still locked against my will under Zell's.

"Excellent sermon, Dr. Hayes. I was very moved," Zell spoke quietly looking into my father's eyes. "Would you and Annie be my guest for dinner?" I would like to speak with you further about your comments on the Fallen Angels."

"What do you think Annie? I would love an opportunity to discuss the topic with Zell."

I opened my mouth to say no way, but Zell put painful pressure on my fingers still sitting on top of his arm. My father looked eager to spend more time with Zell. My poor father who saw so little joy since my mother died. Zell, I could tell no all day but not my dad. Dad never asked me for anything, and it was impossible for me to deny him his request. Of course, that is exactly what Zell was counting on.

"Oww . . . K," I exclaimed as Zell dug his nails into my arm. The sound came out as an affirmative statement even though I didn't want it to sound that way. It was the consent for which my dad was waiting.

"Wonderful," Dad beamed.

"Please ride with us, Dr. Hayes," Zell offered.

"It's not every day that I get an opportunity to ride in a Lamborghini. I accept your invitation."

"Excellent," Zell beamed dropping my hand like a hot potato as he put his hand on my dad's back to guide him toward the car. They both ignored me and walked deep in conversation to the waiting Lamborghini. I stood there for a few seconds forgotten. Then, I stomped behind them my heels making quite a racket on the stone walk to the car. Zell held the seat up for me to climb in the backseat. "Annie, ride in the back so that I may continue conversing with your dad on the ride to the restaurant."

If looks could kill, Zell would be falling over dead about now. If my glowering scowl bothered him, he never showed it; instead, he bestowed a lovely smile in my direction. Zell and my dad talked easily all the way to the restaurant. Of course, Zell chose the most elegant restaurant in town. He drove to the covered entrance and tossed the keys to the wide-eyed young valet who was waiting.

"I didn't know Lamborghinis came with a backseat."

"They don't. This is a prototype that hasn't been put into production yet, the Estoque. The auto makers put the production of the Estoque on the back burner while they pursued a sports utility version, so I have one of the few ever made. I also have the sports coupe, but I drove the Estoque this morning hoping you and Annie would be my guests for dinner."

"How interesting," my father cooed.

My dark mood soon vanished as I saw how much my father was enjoying dinner and conversation with Zell. They talked theology, scientific theory, and about several of the great minds of the past. If only my dad knew that Zell had most likely known Da Vinci, Sir Isaac Newton and Einstein and not just studied them; then perhaps, he would not be so enamored of him. Still, I was glad to see they made great companions. Dad has been alone for so long. Even being a pastor, most people simply wanted him as a confidante or a counselor not as a friend. Even Jon saw him as an obstacle not as a person. I relaxed and began to enjoy dinner with Dad and Zell. Zell really was a charmer and regaled Dad and I with many humorous antidotes.

"What does your father do?" Dad asked Zell.

"My father?"

"Yes, and your mother how is she?"

"My mother died in childbirth when I was thirteen."

"I am so sorry to hear that. It is very unusual nowadays for a woman to die in childbirth."

Zell's silver gaze moved to my eyes.

"Your father?" Dad inquired.

"My father taught me at a young age how to fashion swords and knives. You may have heard of the family business, Starr Knives?"

"Starr Knives? Of course, Starr Knives is a household name. The very finest cutlery available."

"Thank you. It is very kind of you to say so."

Thankfully, the waiter brought the check to Zell and squelched any further conversation about Zell's family.

Zell paid for dinner, and we headed toward the church to pick up my dad's car. I asked Dad if I could drive the car back because I wanted to stop by Kate's and return some earrings I borrowed. In reality, I was hoping Zell would be gone when I got home. Zell gave me a worried glance, but he didn't say anything.

Kate wasn't home either. I really wanted to talk to her about everything that had happened this weekend. Disappointed, I dropped the earrings off with her mom and started for home. Of course, when I returned, Zell's obscenely gorgeous car was in the driveway. I think if I had not returned until midnight, he would still have been there waiting.

When I entered the room, Dad and Zell were deeply engrossed in a conversation about Fallen Angels once again. Neither one even looked up when I entered the room. I stood there for several minutes, but neither even looked my way.

"Hey," I yelled. "I'm home."

Zell immediately stood up and acted as though he just realized I was in the room. I knew better. He was ignoring me. My dad, yes, he was an expert at ignoring me. Not Zell, he was aware of my every move. Who was he trying to fool?

"Annie, your dad has given me permission to take you for a drive. Would you like to go?" Zell asked.

"Not really," I shrugged trying to give a little pay back to Zell for neglecting me.

"Annie, go and get some fresh air. You hang around this house too much. Go with Zell," my father begged. I knew this is exactly what Zell was counting on.

"Ah Dad," I whined.

"Please Annie. Go make friends with Zell. You don't go out enough with your friends."

"I'll go only to please you father," I growled scowling at Zell. He turned back to my father.

"It has been a pleasure making your acquaintance, sir." Zell stated taking my father's hand and shaking it.

"I would like to make a request of you sir before I go," Zell began.

"What is your request?" my father asked him.

"I would like to court your daughter," Zell replied seriously.

"Court me?" I echoed amazed.

Zell ignored me completely and waited for my father's response.

"Court me?" I said a little louder this time.

Zell continued to ignore me and met my father's gaze, eyeball to eyeball.

Finally, my father tore his eyes from Zell's beautiful silver ones and looked at me puzzled.

"What do you have to say about this, Annie?" my father asked me.

"I think all this is stupid. That's what I think. This is the twenty-first century, and you're asking my father if you can court me?"

Zell never looked at me once. He continued to look at my father.

"Annie, do you or do you not want to date this young man?" Dad asked me.

Slowly, Zell turned his silver stare on me.

"Or not," I answered. "Zell, this is all unnecessary. We can hang out as friends," I said as nonchalantly as possible even though I was sure my dad and Zell could hear how wildly my heart was beating.

"Annie, the term, hang out, would be disrespectful to you. I don't need someone to play pool with. I want you as my girlfriend. I want to date you with your father's blessing," Zell said seriously.

My father looked at me raising one eyebrow as if in a question smugly grinning because he knew I had met my match. I hated it when he did that. It was like he was asking, "Well young lady, what do you have to say for yourself?" Instead, he said, "Finally, a young man that will show my daughter the respect that she, and all women, deserve."

I huffed looking from my father to Zell. I was surprised that my dad wasn't pulling out what hair he had left screaming, "Yes, of course you can court her." All of this was so corny. But then, this was Zell's style. If he did anything, he did it in the appropriate way—beyond reproof. I crossed my arms and huffed again.

"Never," I said almost gagging on the words.

"Annie?" Zell gave me a look, and I knew he was not pleased with my response. "Never is a long time, trust me."

"Oh, Ok. You win. I agree. I will c . . . c . . . court Zell and anyone else that I choose." It was all I could do to stutter it out. It all sounded so lame. I added that last part about anyone else that I chose just to irritate Zell.

"In that case Zell, you have my blessing to court my daughter," my father adjusted his glasses nervously as he spoke, but I knew he was ready to flip a few cartwheels. "And anyone else you may choose young lady will be dealt with on a case by case basis." I knew it! Zell already had my dad wrapped around his little finger.

"Thank you sir. I promise you that I will be good to Annie and protect her always."

I rolled my eyes feeling nauseated.

"Good grief, Zell. Knock it off. You sound like you are asking for my hand in marriage," I said exasperated.

"I wasn't going to do that just yet. If you want, sweetheart, I will be honored to ask your father for permission to marry you." Zell winked at Dad over my head unknown to me.

"Ahhhhhh!" I yelled. Gritting my teeth, I stomped to my bedroom and slammed the door and threw myself on the bed.

A few minutes later, I heard a soft knock on the door.

"Annie?" It was Zell's voice.

"What?" I yelled.

"It's a nice day. Let's go for that ride in the convertible," Zell pleaded.

I pulled a pillow over my head and didn't answer.

"Annie?" Zell's voice came through the door again. "Please."

"Oh, Ok," I groaned dragging myself off the bed. I didn't really want to lie around the house all day anyway, especially when there was a convertible sitting in my driveway. "I'll be out as soon as I change."

I went to the closet and tossed my heels in a box. Then I let the pink dress fall to the floor. I tossed jeans, slacks, skirts, dresses, sweaters, and tee-shirts one right after one another in the floor looking for something to wear. Zell was always perfectly dressed. I wanted to look perfect too.

"Hmmp, fat chance of that happening," I growled. I was just too much of a tomboy. I didn't have perfect clothes. Nor, had I ever wanted them until this moment. Finally, I settled for a newer pair of jeans, a black tee-shirt with my favorite band plastered all over the front, and black and silver glittery flip flops. I twisted my hair up and put a silver clip in it.

"Let's go," I growled at Zell when I entered the room where my dad and Zell still deep in discussion sat talking.

"Certainly," Zell rose to his feet and shook my father's hand. "It has been wonderful to meet you sir, and I look forward to seeing you often in the future," Zell said for my benefit.

"Anytime, Zell," my father gushed back.

"Add another conquest to Zell's long list of groupies," I said aloud staring at my dad in disbelief.

I stomped out the door leaving Zell behind. Zell grinned at my dad and shrugged. Dad laughed.

"Good luck, son," Dad wished him still laughing.

I was sitting in the passenger's seat buckled in when Zell made it out of the door.

"Do you mind if we go by my house, so I can change?" Zell asked.

"No," I grunted.

"Why are you always in a bad mood when I'm around?"

"It's just you wind everyone around your little finger. It's getting disgusting."

"Would you rather I made them hate me? Maybe, I could flip my wings up, and let them see me for the monster I truly am."

Instantly, I was remorseful. "You are not a monster," I replied looking out the window. I didn't want to meet his eyes. I suddenly felt like I would cry.

Within twenty minutes we were at Zell's lake house.

"I'll just sit here by the lake while you change."

I was mesmerized by the beauty and calming effect of the lake even though the last time I saw the lake there was a vampire standing knee deep in it.

Zell stood very still listening and smelling the air.

"Everything should be fine. You'll be safe here while I change. I won't be but a few minutes." Zell headed for the house taking off the coat of his suit as he walked.

It was a warm, sunny afternoon. The big meal, the warm sun, and the sound of lapping water relaxed me, and within minutes my eyes began to feel heavy. I'm not sure how long I slept, but when I awoke Zell was watching me from the chair next to mine

"It's pleasant to sleep," he said quietly. "You look so beautiful and peaceful when you sleep. I could watch you for hours."

"Don't be silly," I yawned stretching. "Why would you want to do that?"

"I've waited on you for so long. I can't get enough of being with you or just looking at you. I'm sorry if I seem forward at times, but believe me, I have no agenda other than keeping you alive and spending as much time with you as possible."

"Yeah, right, six thousand years of waiting, I believe you said." I still didn't buy into the idea that Zell was six thousand years old. He looked to be late teens at a stretch maybe twenty.

"I used to look younger, but I have aged some since you have been born. I have been careful all my life to get enough rest so that when you were born, I could not sleep and age, yet still not be too old for you. The night we spent at the island together was the first time I've slept in seventeen years. "

"That's impossible."

"With me, it's very possible, even a fact."

"How can you go without sleeping?" I asked still not believing him.

"I just don't require it. I can sleep if I want. However, if I go for long periods without sleeping, it ages me. I've aged probably two human years in the last seventeen years you've been alive, because I refused to sleep. I still don't age as fast as a 100% human would, but I do age when I am sleep-deprived."

"And you haven't slept but once in seventeen years because you have been watching and protecting me. Is that what you expect me to believe?" I indicated with the tone of my voice that I didn't believe him for a second.

"It's just the way it is, Annie, whether you believe it or not."

I jumped to my feet wanting to change the subject.

"Let's go for that ride now."

"Let's," Zell smiled and took my hand.

It was heavenly speeding down I-85 with the top down on Zell's sports car. He had exchanged the Estoque for his two seater sports car while I slept. The weather was perfect—a warm, spring afternoon.

"Where are we going?" Zell asked.

"Let's go downtown and walk around," I suggested.

I closed my eyes and imagined I was back at Zell's island fortress.

"What are you thinking about?" Zell asked me.

"I was wondering what you have been doing the last six thousand years."

"Waiting for you," Zell answered solemnly.

"No, really, what kind of things have you done? Six thousand years is a long time to fill up with activities."

"I took the one thing my father gave me, the knowledge to fashion knives and swords from metal, and I made a business of it. I have sold my swords and knives to knights, kings, and militaries throughout the ages. King Richard and Lancelot fought with my swords, and I fought by their side. King Richard even knighted me for my valor in battle. You may call me Sir Zell if you wish. Have you ever heard of the Sword of Excalibur?"

"You did not. You didn't make Excalibur! "

"I am a very talented blade smith. Who do you think thrust Excalibur into that Rock?" Zell laughed.

"Is that how you have made your money?" I asked.

"When you have a business that has lasted for thousands of years, you make a dollar or two." Zell laughed. "Seriously, I have so much that I don't know what to do with it all. I have many charities that I completely fund. I have money invested and banked all over the world. Lionel, my assistant, keeps track of it. His sister, Isadora, runs my household and keeps everything going. They are descendants of a family that has cared for me through the centuries. Isadora's son, Lionel the XXXVIII is in college now. He is majoring in business. He will work in my company, Starr Cutlery, until his uncle dies. Then he will take his place in my home as my assistant."

"Lionel, the thirty-eighth?" I laughed. Zell laughed too.

"Yes, they don't show much variety in names."

"Why? Why would a family dedicate itself to you throughout the ages?"

I saw clouds of darkness veil his eyes as he began to relate Lionel's story. "I saved the original Lionel and his father from an early death many, many years ago." Zell had pulled his car over at the curb and parked. "How about a coffee, and I'll tell you the rest of the story."

"That sounds great," I answered truly interested in hearing the rest of his story. We didn't immediately head for the coffee shop. Instead, we investigated all the shops along the road in the artsy district of Atlanta. Zell took my hand, and we wandered in and out of shops and wove in and out of artists who sat on the sidewalk painting for patrons who posed for them, or we watched curiously over their shoulder while they painted for a patron. I talked Zell into posing with me for an artist. Reluctantly, he did so. He didn't seem to like having his picture made or painted.

I hadn't noticed that the artist was drawing caricatures. Zell and I both laughed uncontrollably when the artist finished. The artist captured the strong lines of Zell's jaw line and had exaggerated them. Overblown muscles bulged from the shirt that the artist had drawn on Zell. The artist drew me with hair wildly flowing everywhere in the portrait. Pouting, full lips, and big, wide blue eyes stared back at me from the caricature. The comical thing was that the artist had drawn beautiful wings on my back.

I laughed so hard that I thought I could barely catch my breath.

"You put the wings on the wrong person," I gasped telling the artist of his mistake laughing until tears rolled down my face. Zell bent over clutching his waist laughing at the ridiculous portrait. The artist was totally confused looking first at me and then at Zell trying to understand the joke.

Zell stood up trying to quell the laughter and patted the man on the back.

"Thank you. I love your masterful interpretation of us." Zell said as he pulled his wallet from his pocket and handed the artist a fistful of hundred-dollar bills. He reached back in his wallet and gave the artist another handful of bills. "Would you make another just like it? I would like for both of us to have one. I love it," Zell said again holding it up to look closer.

Apparently, the artist no longer cared what the joke was about. He laughed too, while holding a wad of hundreds in his fist. Zell promised to return tomorrow and pick up the portraits. He took my hand, and we walked a short distance to the coffee shop still trying to compose ourselves. Zell ordered a couple of cappuccinos, and we found a secluded little table underneath the only tree in the small dining area near the street.

"Go on. Finish your story," I urged Zell eagerly.

"Lionel was a first cousin of King Arthur. King Arthur left him in command when he went to fight the Saxons in the Battle of Mt. Badon. Mordred, son of Arthur's half-sister, Morgause, attempted to kill Lionel and his father, and would have been successful if I had not intervened and fought off the assassins. It was Mordred's intention to take the throne from Arthur while he was away in battle. There were rumors that Mordred was Arthur's illegitimate son and felt the kingdom was his. I never asked Arthur if the rumors were true, sometimes I wish I had asked.

Anyway, Lionel and his father were so grateful to me for saving their lives that they never left my side after that. Throughout the generations, the first-born son has always been named Lionel and raised to care for me, my home, and my fortune. I never asked it of any of them. I have tried to stop them, but it is no use. They are not servants. I have made their families very wealthy. They could go their own way at any time, but yet they have all chosen to stay. I am grateful to them all.

That faraway, sad look that I was becoming accustomed to came back to Zell's eyes.

"I thought King Arthur was only a legend," I said quietly patting Zell's hand that lay on the table.

"Most legends are based in truth. King Arthur was very real, an incomparable warrior. It is said that in one battle, he killed hundreds of the barbaric Saxons with his own hand." Zell laughed. "Actually, it took both our hands that day."

"You fought with King Arthur?" I asked in awe.

"Aye, at his side," Zell answered quietly. I have fought alongside good men against evil throughout history. I could have killed Hitler once. We were standing face to face. I have made it my duty to assist though, so I led others to him. They cut him off from his troops, and that is when he committed suicide."

"Why did you not kill him when you had the chance?"

"King Herod, Mordred, Vlad III the Impaler, you know him as Count Dracula, Stalin, Ivan the Terrible, Hitler, and countless other evil rulers, I have encountered them all. Was it to be my face and name to show up throughout history as the avenger which killed all these monsters? That would have been a little suspicious, don't you think? I don't think I could have escaped notoriety. I would have become a superhero type, and that is not my mission. My mission is you."

"I can see your point, and yet I feel kind of guilty for some reason. Is it painful to remember all the people you have known, loved, and had to watch die?"

"More than you can know. There have been thousands of people I have been very fond of. I have helped bury scores of relatives and people I have loved—always going on alone. Being eternal is not as glorious as you would think. My life has been extremely lonely most of the time. There has been only one true love in my life."

A pang of jealously hit me like a train. Zell had loved someone before and had to watch her grow old and die. I felt sorry for him, but I felt sorry for me too. I don't treat him very well, but I had gotten used to the thought that he belonged exclusively to me. To think there were others hurt a bit, and I fell silent. I wondered if he had been a father. Should I dare to ask him, or would it be too painful for him? I decided not to ask him, but now that the thought had come into my head. It would not let me rest. I had to know who she was, and if they married. I had to know if Zell had been a father and had to bury his own children. I felt so rotten for being mean to him when all he has ever done is be kind to me and protective.

"Would it be too painful to tell me about her?" I asked taking Zell's hand in my own.

"Tell you about who?" Zell asked puzzled.

"Your one true love," I whispered leaning close to him.

"Ah, her," he smiled dreamily.

"What was she like? Did you have a child? Tell me about her please," I begged Zell quietly.

Zell glanced away, and I thought for a moment that the memories were too painful for him to talk about. After long seconds of staring into the street, he turned back to me and sighed.

"She was the most beautiful woman whom I have ever seen in my six thousand years of life. She had such an energy about her. We had so much fun together, and I was devoted to her."

"Awe," I murmured feeling my heart twist a bit. "Did you marry her? Were you a father?" I could not keep the questions inside me any longer. I had to know if Zell had loved her enough to marry her.

"No, we didn't marry, though I wanted to marry her," he sighed looking incredibly sad. "I wanted children too, but she would not marry me," he shook his head sadly.

"Why Zell? Why wouldn't she marry you? Didn't she love you back?" I asked tears coming to my eyes at the thought of his unrequited love.

"She didn't feel about me the same way that I felt about her. I believe the way she put it was 'I creeped her out.' She equated me to a nightmare. She thought that I was a stalker and a psycho. Yes, those were her words precisely—a stalker and a psycho. In addition, she is fearful of having to swim through the drool of my admirers if she chose to be with me," he added his voice breaking as he tried to hold in his laughter.

"Oh! You are rotten," I growled pushing his hand which I had been holding back in his direction.

"Alas, now I am a rotting corpse in addition to being a stalker and a psycho," he chuckled.

"Come on, let's swing by the zoo," I said jumping to my feet and pulling Zell up deciding to change the subject. "There's a big gorilla there who reminds me of you."

Zell's mood lifted. He smiled and drew me close hugging me.

"Thank you, Annie," he whispered.

"For what," I said puzzled.

"For being the light in my otherwise dark existence," Zell replied.

"We'll see if you still feel that way after putting up with me for a couple of months," I laughed.

"I will," Zell whispered still holding me close. "I meant it you know. You are my one true love. There has never been anyone else."

"You flatter me. I don't think I'm worth a six thousand year wait."

"No," Zell whispered pulling back and lifting my chin. "You are worth much more than that."

"Come on now. The zoo awaits." I wiggled in his arms trying to escape. I didn't want Zell or anyone else promising me their undying love.

Reluctantly, Zell released me holding on only to my hand. We walked the short distance to the zoo. We spent the rest of the afternoon wandering around the zoo arm in arm. We were enjoying ourselves so much that it was already dark when we left the zoo. Zell's light-hearted mood changed, and I could feel his mood swing as if it were a tangible object.

"What is it?" I asked.

"I can feel evil close by," Zell answered in a low tone.

"Is it a Dark One?" I asked clutching Zell's arm.

"I don't think so," Zell answered looking into the dark night. I could feel rather than see him begin to unbutton his shirt.

"Is this why you always wear button up shirts?" I nervously giggled.

"The bulge of my swords underneath a tee-shirt is hard to explain," Zell gave a half-hearted laugh in return.

It was then that we saw them. There were six thuggish-looking guys around Zell's car. Two of them were actually seated inside the convertible.

"I would send you back to the zoo, but it may be a ruse to separate us," Zell said coolly, and continued to walk toward them.

"I wouldn't leave you even if you ordered me back to the zoo. I'm the reason you are in this mess."

"Stay behind me then," Zell responded looking at me tenderly for a moment, and then he turned facing the men.

"May I help you gentlemen?" Zell called out to them pushing me behind him.

"Yeah man, toss us yo' keys so's we can take yo' car for a ride." The closest one to us was dressed in a tee-shirt about three sizes too big. His cap was turned so that the bill of his cap was over his shoulder. He pulled a gun from the waist band of a baggy pair of jeans.

Zell took out his keys and tossed them at the feet of the thug with a gun. Zell moved me to his other side, his side facing away from the gunman.

"And yo' hoe too."

"The car you can have. The girl stays with me." Zell said sternly.

Evidently, the gang didn't like his answer and the two seated in the car stood up on his leather seats and jumped out while the closest one with a gun quickly crossed the space between us and the car holding his gun out at eye level shaking it at us. He stopped three feet in front of me holding the gun across from my forehead. The rest of his posse pulled weapons and moved in our direction. I could feel Zell stiffen beside me.

The guy with the gun in front of me waved the gun in my face threatening to kill me in the most vulgar language I had ever heard. I was dead. I knew I was dead, or they would shoot Zell and take me with them. I was sure when they finished with me that I would be dead too.

Zell moved like lightning. I heard material ripping and the faint, yet somehow familiar, metallic scrape as he pulled the swords out from underneath his shirt. I saw the gunman's hand with the gun still grasped in it separate from his body and fall to the ground as if in slow motion. Zell twirled like a deadly top swords flashing in the light from the street lamps. The gunman who was not much more than a kid, maybe eighteen or nineteen, grabbed his arm where the hand had been seconds earlier and fell to the ground screaming. Blood streamed into pools around his writhing figure on the ground.

In an instant, Zell's wings snapped out and covered us as bullets began to hit the wings and fall with little pings to the ground. It became silent as the clips were emptied. Zell reacted quickly, withdrawing his wings and simultaneously throwing both swords. On each end of the group, two gunmen were knocked backward into the street impaled as the swords sank deep into their chests coming out of their backs. He drew the sword with the flame, and leapt across the parking lot in the blink of an eye decapitating the next closest thug with it. There was no blood. The sword cauterized the cut as it sliced through the flesh cutting off the blood flow. The gunman blinked twice, and then his head slowly rolled from his shoulders and across the road a few feet. The two thugs which were left backed up so fast that their baggy pants tripped them as they tried to retreat. Zell grabbed the one to his left and threw him across a five-lane road where he landed against a brick building. I could hear the crunch of bone as his head flattened like the bottom of an iron as it hit. The thug slid slowly to the ground leaving a trail of blood, bone, and flesh on the building as he slithered down the brick wall. The remaining carjacker began to scream.

"Stop," I yelled as Zell advanced toward the gangster who was left standing. Zell hesitated. "Leave this one for a witness."

Stepping around Zell, I faced the one that had escaped the mayhem.

"Put your gun down, or I will release him to finish you," I shouted. The gunman quickly did as he was told and laid the gun on the ground falling to his knees as he did so.

"Please don't let him kill me," he whimpered.

"Count yourself blessed," I spat at him. "Go back and tell others like your friends lying here that any evil from this point on will be met with swift justice, not from the law, but from this avenging angel." I pointed to Zell and turned just slightly. I gasped when I looked at Zell. The very sight of him scared me silly. He was at his full height maybe twelve or thirteen feet tall. His white enormous wings which were outlined in bold black and silver feathers were stiff and erect. He was splattered with blood and held a metal sword that he had retrieved from the bodies in one hand and the flaming sword in the other. His shirt had ripped from his body as he shape-shifted to his full height, and his trousers from the thigh down were ripped into shreds. His face, no longer warm and teasing, was as stone. His eyes were piercing and dark, no longer the warm silver color that I loved. The cool, night breeze blew his long, golden hair gently around his stone face. I was in shock and awe. I had never seen him in a full warrior state before, and he was beyond frightening. He had fought like a Trojan. It was obvious that he was not of this world. It was then that I knew beyond a shadow of doubt Zell was everything he said he was, and he spoke the truth about himself and my destiny. I began to shake uncontrollably. I tried to pull myself together. Turning my back to him and breathing heavily, I faced the punk in front of me.

"Take a good look at him. If you *ever* commit an evil act again, he will find you. There will not be a jail cell with free meals, a judge, or a jury. There will not be life behind bars with cable television and workout equipment. You will be dead. Your life is no longer your own. You must compensate for all the evil you have done. You must tell others that evil will be met with his sword. You must spend the remainder of your life helping those you have victimized, helping the helpless, telling of this night and how your life was spared, or he *will* find you!"

I saw the blue lights of a squad car several blocks away.

"The police are coming. Run to them. Tell them your story. If you sway from the truth, I promise he will find you and finish you off."

With those final words, the thug jumped up and ran waving his arms down the middle of the street toward the police car. Zell scooped up his keys from where they lay beside the gunman with one hand lying unconscious in his own blood. I noticed he was a more normal size, and his swords had been returned to their sheaths. The color had returned to his face, and his eyes were once more silver. He heaved a great sigh and smiled at me with his beautiful smile.

"Let's go Annie," Zell said quietly grabbing my hand and moving me toward the Lamborghini.

We jumped in, and Zell gunned the engine burning rubber as we left the scene.

We traveled for a few miles in silence. When Zell spoke, I was terrified at his words.

"So it begins," he stated quietly.

"What begins?" I asked him.

"Your destiny," he replied calmly, "and mine."

8. HEADLINES

SOMETHING WAS CHASING ME. I WAS running through a forest stumbling over roots, rocks, and rotting logs. Terrified, blood pounded in my head and ears. Whatever it was, it was getting closer. I could hear it coming after me thrashing in the undergrowth. Trembling, I started to sob. Where was Zell, my protector? Why wasn't he here? I tripped over a small boulder and hit the soft, damp earth that smelled of decaying leaves. I could feel it behind me. I turned and rolled over on my back. When I saw the monster that stood over me, it frightened me more than a hundred demons could. Zell stood over me with a sword drawn ready to plunge it in through my heart. It was the Zell of the night at the Zoo when he fought with the thugs. His cold, dark eyes and stone face revealed none of the tenderness of the past. He was huge—a killing machine. Only this time his victim was me. He raised his sword ready to plunge it into my heart.

"No, Zell, don't," I sobbed.

Strong arms picked me up and cradled me. Someone rocked me back and forth whispering through my hair and into my ear. I must have been having another nightmare because now I was back in my room in my bed.

"Shhhh, Annie, shhhh."

I knew that voice. I would know it anywhere. In any dimension, in any universe, in any age past or present, I would know that voice. It was Zell. Not the stone cold Zell with dark eyes, but my Zell, the gentle giant, with the warm silver eyes. He was rocking me back and forth in his arms, like a mother does her babe. Lightly, his lips touched mine for the briefest of moments. My breathing became more even, and I drifted back off to a dreamless sleep.

I woke with my alarm clock spouting the news.

"In a late-night car-jacking attempt, five alleged carjackers died as the car owner fought back. The lone surviving carjacker identified the potential victim as a gigantic winged creature with swords. One carjacker was decapitated in the incident. Police are hunting for the silver sports car owner and a blond teenage female to collaborate the survivor's story."

My eyes opened wide, but I was frozen. I didn't think about the story hitting the news. I jumped up, and ran to my closet grabbing a new blue jean skirt that I had never worn and a long-sleeve tee-shirt with the word Pink written in sequins. Yanking my drawer open, I pulled out clean underwear not bothering to shut the drawer. All I could think of was getting to school early to talk to Zell. I showered and hurriedly pulled on my clothes. I was in a hurry, but I didn't want to look like a bag lady next to the perfection of Zell. I brushed my hair and went to look for a pair of shoes to match my tee-shirt when I heard the doorbell ring. Panicking, I was sure it was the police. They have come to arrest me as an accessory to murder. I knew my dad would answer the door, and I hurried to put on my shoes. I ran to the front door where, just as I had thought, my dad stood with the door open. I heard low murmurs. I flattened against the wall in the hallway and groaned. I wondered if you were allowed to wear flip flops in prison. I just knew I would not look good in an orange prison jumpsuit. I closed my eyes trying to figure out what to say in the interrogation.

"Miss Hayes, where were you around nine o'clock Sunday evening?" I could hear them now.

"Annie? Annie Hayes what are you doing pressed against the wall with your eyes closed?" my dad asked.

"Nothing, just resting," I answered cracking one eye lid a bit.

"Resting? Annie, you have been behaving in a most bizarre manner lately," Dad related worriedly.

"Ever the drama queen," I breathed smiling slightly.

"Pull yourself together. Zell is in the living room waiting to take you to school," Dad stated.

"Zell?" I questioned, "Not the police?"

"The police? Annie what are you talking about?" Dad asked.

"Just kidding," I half snorted and half laughed.

"Bizarre," Dad mumbled shaking his head as he walked away.

I hurried into the living room where Zell was casually sprawled on the couch.

"Have you heard the news?" I whispered.

"No, but I have seen the headlines," Zell retorted smiling at me.

"Headlines? Oh God, we're going to jail," I moaned sliding down into the nearest chair.

"We're not going to jail, Annie."

"Yes, we are. Yes, we are," I moaned dropping my chin on my chest and shaking my head up and down.

"Get your books. Let's get in the car so we can talk," Zell said quietly pulling me to my feet.

I picked up my books and purse from the table by the door and walked silently behind Zell to the car.

Zell started to open the door for me, but he paused laughing.

"What's so funny?" I asked him.

"Where do you get the shoes that you wear?" he laughed barely containing himself.

"What's wrong with them?" I replied stopping to look down at my pink sequined sneakers. "They match my tee shirt."

"I love them. They are so Annie," he laughed.

I gave him a half grin and slid in.

Zell stopped at the deli down the street from school. He came out with a coffee for each of us, a bagel for me, and a newspaper. He drove to school and parked in the empty lot. We were an hour early for school. I took a bite of my bagel, and he opened the paper and read. "Ten-Foot Foot Avenging Angel Decimates Local Hoodlums." I groaned and slid down in my seat, but I did not ask him to stop reading.

"Atlanta's police report that about nine thirty p.m., six carjackers accosted a couple leaving the Atlanta Zoo. An eye-witness reports that when the assailants pulled guns on the couple and fired, a winged figure killed two of the carjackers by throwing swords through their hearts. A third would be carjacker bled to death en route to a nearby hospital when his hand holding a gun on the victims was severed from his body. A fourth carjacker was thrown seventy-five feet into a brick building crushing his skull. The fifth assailant was decapitated by some unknown weapon. The lone survivor reports that the person that fought off the assailants possessed superhuman strength and was a giant man with wings. Police are looking for a female witness who left the scene in a silver sports car. The lone surviving carjacker is being held by police. This bizarre attack has police baffled and unsure of whom they are looking for in this incident—hero, villain, or creature."

"Zell, will they find us?" I asked not looking up from the bagel I held in my lap.

"I don't see any ten foot winged creatures around here."

"But they know what I look like."

"It appears to me that the only description they have is of a blonde-headed teenage female. That narrows it down to about fifty thousand potential witnesses in the Atlanta area. The only place that harbors more blonde teenagers in the United States is Southern California. Don't worry, Annie, no one is going to come looking for us."

I sighed, "I guess you're right."

"Just don't talk about this with anyone, Annie. Not even Kate," Zell said seriously.

"I won't. I can't. I still find it hard to believe."

"Let's just try our best to forget it," Zell said calmly sipping his coffee.

"I can't forget it Zell. Five young men died last night."

"Evil young men, Annie."

"But still . . ." I paused.

"Annie, it was them or us."

"But the way they died."

"They had guns, Annie. I had swords. They were not at a disadvantage. They wanted the car. I tossed them the keys to a $450,000 car. Then they wanted you. Was I to toss them you, too?"

"No, but . . . ."

"No buts, Annie, you can't have it both ways. We may not have survived. They were evil. They wanted blood. They would take the spoils: money, jewelry, the car, your virginity, and next your life. I have seen their kind all through history. They want nothing but to destroy and kill."

"I know you're right, but it still feels wrong,"

"Of course, it does. It is never an easy thing to take someone's life. You cannot combat evil with compassion though, Annie. All you can do is eradicate it. I gave them a chance to take the car and go. They chose death. They didn't even want a fight. They just wanted to slaughter us. If it had not been us, Annie, there would be two innocent people dead this morning at the hands of those evil men. They just happened to pick on the wrong couple. Their bad, not ours."

"May I ask you another question?" I asked.

Zell turned looking at me, "Of course."

"I had a nightmare last night. You were chasing me, trying to kill me."

"It was only a dream. I would never harm you."

"Were you in my bedroom last night?"

"Yes," Zell replied.

"Why?" Annie asked.

"I stand guard over you every night. In fact, every night since your birth."

"Have I always been in that much danger?"

"Yes, I have saved your life countless times. I have been there every night of your life watching you sleep. It's my favorite part of the day," Zell looked at me and smiled. He reached over and cupped my face in his hand. "You are so beautiful when you sleep, and your mouth is closed."

"I'll show you mouth," I raised my voice and smacked Zell's hand away, but I burst into tears and threw my arms around Zell's neck. Zell held me until my tears subsided.

"I'm sorry. I seem to be a bundle of nerves lately. I'm not going to make a very good heroine as my destiny plays out if I live that long," I said brokenly as I wiped at my face with the napkin that came with my bagel. "Can I ask something of you Zell?"

"Of course."

"Will you stop coming to my bedroom at night? I do need some privacy."

"No, I can't," he said simply.

"Why not?"

"Annie, you are in danger with every breath. I don't talk about it much because I want you to live your life as normally as possible. I am here to take care of the 'problems' as they arise. The attacks are increasing that is why I have revealed myself to you. If I was not constantly around, I think the Dark Ones would be bolder, and their attacks more frequent. I don't want you to worry. I want you to live your life. I never invade your privacy. I always wait close by until you are asleep."

"I'll never have a normal life again."

"Perhaps someday you will. When you have fulfilled your destiny, the Dark Ones will no longer hunt you. They are trying to eradicate you before you expose their evil kingdom."

"How do you get in my room?" I asked suddenly turning the conversation. "You can't walk through walls, can you?"

"No," Zell snorted, "I could burst through them but not walk through them. Have you ever heard of Harry Houdini?" Zell asked glad to leave the subject of the Dark Ones as well.

"The magician, or illusionist, or whatever he was?" I returned his question with a question.

"He was a friend of mine. He taught me all his escape artist tricks in exchange for a few of my swords. He taught me an invaluable skill. Sometimes, a warrior needs to be able to slip in and out of an area. Sometimes, a warrior needs to escape and live to fight another day. Harry taught me everything I needed to know about stealth and escape. He was only 5 feet 5 inches tall. He loved my height. I transformed for him once. Thinking it an illusion, he hounded me for years to teach him my secret. I could never convince him that it was real and not an illusion."

The bell rang for students to enter the building. Together we climbed out of the car and headed for homeroom. Luckily, Jon was not in any of my classes. The only time I saw him was at lunch. Kate, however, was in most of them. She sat down in the seat in front of me.

"Have you heard the news?" Kate asked excitedly.

"About the beheading?" I replied.

"Uweee, no, about Austin and I," Kate giggled dangling her left hand in front of my face. On her ring finger was Austin's, I presume, class ring. Kate had layered rows of tape around the ring to make it fit her finger.

"Nice," I groaned and looked at Zell rolling my eyes.

"So," Kate whispered conspiratorially loudly smacking her gum and leaning toward me, "What did you two do this weekend?"

Zell looked at me and cocked an eyebrow waiting for my answer.

"Do you really want to know what we did this weekend?" I whispered back leaning closer to Kate.

"Aahhh, yeaaah," Kate drawled out the words in true southern belle tradition.

"On Friday after we left school, Zell flew us to his private island. Not on a plane, he simply sprouted wings and flew us there," I whispered flapping my arms. "He has spent hundreds of years building and perfecting everything on the island just for me. It is beautiful. It's full of flowers and waterfalls. Then, he cooked for me, and we ate in front of the fire in his stone cottage. He sang to me for hours. We spent the night there and swam with dolphins the next day on his private beach. On Saturday, we flew home literally flying through the air via Zell's wings. You know about the cookout, but what you don't know is that I was attacked by a vampire on Lauren's beach. Zell fought him off, and I killed the dirty vamp with an umbrella pole through his back." I demonstrated with an imaginary pole in my hand. "Then, Zell shows up at my house on Sunday morning, meets my father and goes to church with me where we play tug of war with my hand all during my dad's sermon. On Sunday afternoon, we went to the Artsy District downtown, had coffee, went to the zoo, but we were attacked. Luckily, Zell is six thousand years old and always carries a few swords on him. He fought off all the bad guys, and we headed home. Honestly, that's all we did."

Kate's eyes widened, and her mouth dropped open. She just sat and stared at me for several seconds. With her mouth still gaping, she looked over at Zell who flashed his fabulous smile and nodded in agreement.

"Seriously, Annie you are mental," she complained. "What did you really do?"

"We just went to a movie?" I guessed.

"Annie, I love you, but your social calendar is so lame. The movie I believe."

I was saved from any further conversation because Kate bought the just went to a movie version. Dr. Patty had walked in the classroom and started roll call. I looked over at Zell, shrugged my shoulders, and smiled.

"Kate thinks the news is trite. She never watches or listens to the news. Besides, if she ever figured it out, she would never betray me," I whispered to Zell smiling.

Zell returned my smile, and I felt the warmth from it begin to spread throughout my body. Thoughts from the weekend cluttered my head. One second I would be smiling to myself thinking about the time we spent together on the island. The next my brow would be furrowed as I recalled the events of last night. I could feel Zell watching me. I was relieved when the bell rang, and I could get up.

Several people crowded around to introduce themselves, mostly girls, of course. Zell dazzled them with his impeccable manners, his charm, and his incomparable good looks. Then, there was his smile. I wasn't the only one who was captivated by that smile. Savanna, Leeann, Lauren, Holly, Rylee, Connor, they all audibly would sigh when he turned his smile toward them. Sickening. Just sickening. Was I a little jealous? I really didn't know why I should be. I told myself that he was just being polite.

When class ended my classmates pressed forward to speak to Zell, and I was pushed further and further to the outskirts of the circle. I finally gave up and huffed off to class. I had already paired up with Matthew when Zell came in the classroom. Zell strolled over to our lab table and leaned against it.

"Hey, I'm new around here, Zell Starr," he introduced himself all friendly-like extending his hand to shake Matthew's.

"Matthew Cavitt," Matthew replied shaking Zell's hand in return. "We met at Lauren's the other night."

"Oh yes, I remember. Look, I need to speak to Annie. Do you think I could be her partner today?" Zell asked sliding a folded one hundred-dollar bill under Matthew's other hand that was resting on the table. Matthew looked down at the bill and hopped up at once.

"Sure thing," he gushed.

I gave both an exasperated look.

"I'll give you a hundred to stay put," I huffed giving Zell a nasty look.

"Two hundred," Zell locked on my eyes.

"Two ten," I ground out desperately searching my memory to see if I had that much left in my trust fund account. I did do a lot of shoe shopping this month.

"Five hundred dollars," Zell stated coolly. "Give up Annie. You can't win the money game with me."

"You're ridiculous," I snorted.

Zell slid onto the stool next to me. He slid his hand in his pocket and pulled out neatly folded bills. He slid them under Matthew's hand.

"Did you have to do that?" I asked Zell.

"What?"

"Buy him off with money," I answered.

"Like I said, I'll never be able to spend all the money I have. I enjoy giving it away."

"Hey, man," Matthew interrupted, "I can't take your money." Matthew slid all the money back across the table.

"Seriously, keep it, pass it forward, do whatever you want with it."

"Nah man, I wouldn't feel right taking your money."

"Really, I want you to have it, please. Just keep it on the down low OK?" Zell whispered looking around.

Matthew's jaw hung open. Slowly, he looked from Zell to me and back at Zell. After a few, long, awkward seconds, he walked away looking puzzled.

"Matt's a good guy. He would have moved without the payoff."

"True, but now he can take his girlfriend out to dinner Saturday night."

"Give me a break," I replied turning my back on him.

"We could double-date on Saturday. That way I could pay for all our dinners, and Matthew could keep his money."

I didn't answer as I listened to Dr. Patty's instructions for the lab.

"Class, today you are going to identify the parts of an egg and examine how the egg has adapted to support the embryo," Dr. Patty began. "Your materials and lab instructions are beside the hand lens on your lab tables. Please begin."

I picked up the lab sheet and began reading.

"First, crack and open the egg carefully placing it in a Petri dish," I read. "Be my guest," I remarked as I slid the egg and Petri dish toward Zell. Zell accommodated cracking open the egg and letting the contents slide into the Petri dish.

"Disgusting." I was not an egg fan. "Second, draw a diagram of the egg, identifying and labeling the main structures of the egg."

"Just read. I'll do the rest," Zell ordered, and he began to draw the diagram on our lab sheet.

"Locate the germinal disk. This is usually a white dot in the center of the yolk. Use a ruler to measure the diameter of the germinal disk. Gross," I grumbled picking up the ruler, holding it daintily between two fingers, and dangling it in front of Zell until he took it from me.

"Locate the Chalazae, the two dense, chord like white structures."

"I've got them," Zell answered pointing toward the Chalazae for me with the end of his pencil.

"Revolting, I'll never eat eggs again," I complained reading on. "Note the consistency of the albumin. What is the major constituent of the albumin?" I dropped the lab sheet. "I'm seriously going to vomit."

Zell looked at me strangely. "Egg white or albumin contains approximately 40 different proteins. Sixty-four percent is ovalbumin. There is nothing really revolting about it." Zell answered as he wrote it down. "You'll be OK, or should I kiss you here in the middle of Biology Lab to settle your stomach?" Zell asked wickedly.

"What part of the egg acts as the placenta in mammals?" I continued ignoring his remark. Zell wrote furiously keeping up with my questions.

"Last question. What will the germinal disk develop into?"

"A baby chick," Zell answered drawing a baby chick rather than writing down the words.

"Cute," I moaned feeling rather nauseated. I looked around and noticed we were the first ones to finish. I laid my head down on the lab table with a thud.

Dr. Patty came around to check on us not believing we were already finished. Zell held out our lab sheet for his inspection. It was unbelievable. It looked professionally done.

"I see. Good work." Dr. Patty congratulated us looking at our work, or Zell's work, in amazement. I closed my eyes and didn't lift my head the rest of class. When the bell rang, we made our way through the throng of girls waiting to talk to Zell to English class.

In English, we were still studying Zell's now-deceased buddy, Shakespeare. I was bored to tears, but Zell got into the class discussion with gusto. I sat back and watched him with interest. He was marvelous. He regaled the class with humorous stories of Shakespeare indicating they were common knowledge in Europe. I knew better. They were most likely personal experiences with Shakespeare. Before I knew it, the bell rang for lunch. Everyone stood and gave Zell a standing ovation. Despite myself, I too, stood and clapped. Zell was an amazing story teller. Of course, if I could believe his wild story, he had about six thousand years to perfect his abilities.

We walked to lunch with a huge group of people. Zell asked what I would like to eat, and I decided I would like a baked potato and salad. He told me to sit, and he would return shortly with my lunch. Within five minutes, he made his way back to our table holding two trays with baked potatoes, salad, and iced tea.

The tables were full, but everyone made room for Zell. I watched Zell eating while he talked and laughed with Matthew and Christopher. He seemed to be totally enjoying himself. I was glad. Zell always seemed so lonely, so friendless, so forsaken. It warmed my heart to see him laughing and joking with other people.

The lunch room was buzzing with news of the would-be carjacking. The girls were afraid there was a monster on the loose. The boys were hoping that there was. Several people were making plans to go to the zoo this weekend and look for what had killed the carjackers. I wanted to tell them not to bother. I wasn't going near downtown, and if I didn't go, there would not be any action. Trouble followed me. Therefore, trouble would be wherever I was, not at the zoo.

Speaking of trouble, here it came. Jon walked through the door of the lunchroom with a smoldering scowl on his face. He saw me and headed straight for our table. Zell was talking with Matthew and Holly, but he must have sensed the atmosphere of the lunch room change. His head snapped up, and he turned to face Jon.

"I need to see you now, outside," Jon commanded.

"Annie, goes nowhere without me," Zell butted in.

Jon took a step toward Zell, and he rose from his seat to meet him.

"Since when does Annie need a guard dog?" Jon remarked insultingly.

Zell towered over him silently glaring at him.

"I'll go see what he wants," I said calmly stepping between them.

"Fine, let's go," Zell replied firmly.

"You're not invited," Jon growled.

"Please Zell, I'll be right outside the door."

"No," he said emphatically, "I go where you go."

The lunchroom became dead silent. Everyone was listening. Heads were bouncing back and forth watching the exchange between Zell, Jon, and me. I didn't know what to do. Neither of them was going to give an inch. Jon moved forward and shoved Zell attempting to push him back down into his seat. Dr. Patty was sitting at the table with Ms. Howard eating lunch. Both turned around when they heard the commotion. Dr. Patty started to get up when he saw Jon shove Zell.

Zell didn't budge. It was as if Jon hit a brick wall. When Zell didn't move, Jon swung at Zell's face. Zell stood still allowing Jon's fist to crunch into his chin. Jon screamed and dropped to his knees holding his fist. Zell never even blinked.

"You broke my fingers," he screamed.

"I did nothing to harm you," Zell replied as if bored with Jon's drama. "Come, Annie, it's time for class." Zell put his arm around me and stepped over Jon, who was still in the floor holding his hand sobbing like a baby. Snickers broke out at first and then full-blown laughter. Jon, the school football hero, and as I was beginning to discern, bully, was humiliated. With a dark look at the laughing crowd seated at the tables, he jumped to his feet and stomped out of the building. Dr. Patty sat back down and resumed eating his lunch. Evidently, Jon wasn't too popular with the teachers because neither moved to see if he was hurt. Ms. Howard smirked and returned to her lunch too.

"That scene looked like something out of Superman," I whispered to Zell.

Zell and I walked the rest of the way in silence to Civics.

"I'm sorry, Annie. I didn't mean to help that idiot make a scene. I just remember what happened last time I let you go off with him at the lake. I was almost too late. Jon can't keep you safe from what hunts you."

I knew what Zell said was true, but it sent chills down my spine.

"What am I going to do? What are we going to do?" I said as my voice quivered.

"We go on as if nothing is wrong. If an attack comes or when an attack comes, I will protect you. Now that you have taken a stand on the side of good, I expect your time will come fairly quickly. I think this weekend that I will teach you how to use a sword. I don't think you would have the strength to kill a Dark One. Unless of course, its back was turned," Zell laughed, but you may be able to hold one off for a while though, if for some reason, we are ever separated." Zell seemed to be mentally making plans already. We took our seats near the back of the classroom. Students began filing in and sweeping the room for a look at Zell. Matthew, Christopher, and Austin came forward to congratulate Zell.

"Thank you for your congratulations, but I didn't want a fight. I just wanted him to leave Annie alone. She has made her choice, and her choice isn't Jon."

Although Zell decried the violence, everyone was still impressed. Jon had been the toughest guy in school up to that point and often a bully until Zell showed up. Civics was boring and uneventful with Ms. Howard lecturing for the full fifty-five minutes. Even Zell was unusually quiet during class. I sat lost in my thoughts trying to pay attention to the lecture, but it was a hopeless battle.

Art class was next. It was an easy elective that I chose to take my senior year. Miss Picknell, my teacher, was talented, fun, and a bulldog for information. Zell had no more than entered the classroom when she pounced.

"My name is Miss Carole Picknell, and I presume that you are the new student?"

Did I imagine it or did Miss Picknell emphasize the Miss in her introduction to Zell?

"Yes, Zell Starr," Zell replied extending his hand to shake hers.

"In fact, you're a very handsome gentleman."

I cocked an eyebrow at Zell. I wasn't sure, but I think he blushed.

"Perhaps you could pose for me one day?" Miss Picknell asked.

Was Miss Picknell flirting with Zell? I thought so.

"Excuse us," I huffed putting my arm through Zell's and pulling him along to a vacant table.

"Am I the only female on earth that doesn't turn to mush over you?" I asked Zell exasperated.

"You're the one person, the only one, that I wish did get mushy over me."

"Don't be ridiculous," I answered quietly as Matthew and Christopher joined us at the art table.

I had been laboring over a painting of a vase of flowers for days. I took out the materials for Zell and myself. Then, I went to get a fresh canvas for Zell. After that, I ignored him as I painted. Zell, Matthew, and Christopher talked quietly all through class. Miss Picknell hovered over them the entire class period. I could have used some help, but I decided I would rather she kept Zell occupied. When she called closing clean-up time, I turned looking at what Zell had done, and it was amazing. He had painted the same vase of flowers as I, but his painting was terrific. He got the colors, shadows, and details just right. He also did it all within the class period.

I threw my brush down, and began putting away my art supplies. Miss Picknell had Zell cornered gushing over his painting. I took the opportunity to get out of class before anyone noticed I was gone. I had a fairly long walk through the halls to the gym and basketball practice. I decided to duck outside and take a shortcut across a back lot, where the recycling dumpsters were kept, to the gym. It was a much shorter trip as the crow flies. However, crows weren't flying today. The sky was overcast and dark. It looked as though the sky would burst at any moment. By the time I reached the dumpsters, I had the feeling of being watched. It began to feel creepy, and I stepped up the pace. I had almost reached the last dumpster when a dark figure stepped out of the shadows from between two dumpsters.

The figure was not human even though it seemed to have two legs and two arms. Big, triangular-shaped red eyes focused on me, and the creature stepped out blocking my path. Its wrinkled, grayish face looked similar to that of a gargoyle, and it crouched on its haunches staring at me. It had wings too, but not the beautiful, large wings that Zell had. The creature had pointy, blackened, spiny looking wings similar to the wings of a bat. It looked like an old, wrinkled, winged man. I froze in my tracks unsure of what to do. Slowly, I began to back up. Keeping my eyes locked with the creature's eyes, I moved one foot backward at a time. The creature didn't move but watched me intently. It opened its wide mouth and hissed at me exposing multiple levels of razor-sharp teeth.

Trembling, I tried to hasten my retreat and stepped on the strap of my book bag. I fell backward hitting my elbows and tearing the flesh from them. I barely noticed the pain though because as I fell the creature leaped for me from his crouching position. It landed a few feet in front of me and hissed again. This time, I had a close-up of those pearly whites. His teeth, rows of them, stuck out in all directions dripping with strands of salvia. A pointed, black tongue darted in and out of his mouth. This creature was so ugly that he would make a train take a dirt road. Shaking, I tried to continue backing up from my seated position further ripping the skin from my elbows in my retreat. In horror, I watched as the creature leaped once again and was flying at me through the air.

From behind me, I heard a swoosh, swoosh, swooshing sound. I looked up and saw a sword flipping end over end toward the creature. The sword hit him with an impact so ferocious that the creature was knocked backwards at least thirty feet through the air. The monster hit the home plate fence on the baseball field and stuck there impaled about six feet off the ground hissing and shrieking. Instantly, Zell was in front of it with his other sword and flaming sword drawn. He plunged the blazing sword deep into the bowels of the creature pulling out the sword that had impaled and nailed the creature to the fence as he did so. The creature burst into flames shrieking hideously. Zell cut off its head as it fell and hurried to my side.

"Let's get out of here," he said quietly helping me up.

The monster continued to shriek for several minutes as it burned even though its head was severed from its body and haunted our escape. Within seconds, we were away from the scene. We walked through the doors that went into the gym.

"If we're lucky, no one saw what just happened," Zell whispered as we walked.

Coach Neely was just inside the gym bouncing a basketball and looking at us strangely.

"What's all that noise coming from outside?" he asked.

Zell and I looked at one another shrugging our shoulders as if we had no idea.

"What's the matter, Annie?" Coach Neely noticed my bleeding elbows and actually sounded concerned.

"I fell out in the parking lot," I replied trying to keep the blood coursing down my arms from getting on my tee-shirt.

"Doesn't look like you'll be playing any basketball today. Go on home and clean that up," Coach Neely said coldly turning his back on us still bouncing the ball. So much for that brief thought that he was concerned. That was a dismissal if I'd ever heard one. As we left the gym, we saw a crowd starting to form around the burning corpse of the creature.

"What is that thing?" I heard Christopher ask Matthew.

Zell and I wasted no time getting as far away from the burning creature as fast as we could.

"Is your coach always so warm and caring?"

"That's pretty much how he always behaves." I groaned as I answered him. The numbness was beginning to wear off, and my elbows were throbbing. When we reached his car, Zell threw our bags in the back seat.

"Let me see how bad you are hurt." Zell inspected my torn flesh. "I'll blow on your wounds and make them feel better."

People always say that, but it does little to assay the pain. However, when Zell blew on my elbows, it was like using one of those numbing sprays. They instantly felt better.

"I need to get you home and clean those wounds for you," Zell advised.

I climbed into his car, and Zell took me home. I apologized all the way home for getting blood all over his seats.

"They're leather. I can wipe it off. No worries."

At home, I went to the closet in the bathroom to get the first-aid kit. Zell cleaned my cuts and scrapes with peroxide then alcohol. He didn't say a word to me the whole time he worked. I watched him as he cleaned the wounds. Was he upset with me for leaving class without him? He must be. He was so unusually quiet, but he was gentle as he worked on my arms and elbows. Everywhere he touched me, my skin felt twenty degrees warmer. I wasn't sure how long I could hold out before I fell madly in love with him. I wanted to touch his face, kiss him, and lay my head on his chest just to listen to his heartbeat. Was I losing my sanity? I had never felt this way about Jon or any other boy, and it was embarrassing and infuriating at the same time.

"Are you mad at me?" I asked him.

"No," he replied not saying another word.

He stayed with me until my father arrived, but he never spoke another word to me unless I asked him a direct question. Dad was at the hospital visiting with a member of the church congregation. Zell rose from the sofa where we had been watching television when my father entered the room.

"Reverend Hayes, Annie fell in the parking lot before basketball practice. Coach Neely told her to skip practice, and I brought her home."

"Is she OK?" I heard Dad ask him.

"She's just a little scratched up, but I cleaned her wounds. She'll be fine. I have to get home. I have some things to take care of, but I may be free to stop by later to check on her if that's permissible," he replied.

Permissible? No teenager in the world talks like that except Zell.

"Of course," Dad agreed.

"Bye, Annie," Zell said quietly, and without even turning to say it to my face, he opened the door and left.

He must be furious with me.

In my dreams that night, I was running through a fog calling for Zell.

"Annie, Annie," Zell called out in return.

I moved toward the sound of his voice, but I still could not find him. I stumbled weeping through the fog. The sound of my sobs echoed in the darkness.

"Annie, stay with your friends. Never be anywhere alone." I could hear Zell's voice whispering through the gray folds of the fog.

"Zell, please don't leave me. I'm sorry," I cried out.

"Everything will be fine. Just don't ever . . . ever go anywhere alone. Stay with your friends. Stay in big crowds. . . Annie," his voice whispered through the fog again.

"Where are you?" I cried out. "Please come back."

For the first time since I have been aware of his presence, Zell was not there when I woke in a heated sweat from my nightmare. I was alone.

9. JON

THE NEXT DAY WAS WORSE. RAIN BLURRED my world to a dull gray like the fog from my nightmares. Reality was even darker. Zell didn't show up at my house the previous night to check on me or the next morning. In a mood as dark as the clouds above, I asked my dad to drive me to school as I had left my Tahoe at school when Zell brought me home. Jon was in my face as soon as I got out of my car.

"What's up Annie? I tried to call you all night."

"Sorry Jonny. I fell outside the gym last night and cut my elbows all up. I went to bed early."

"Who is this guy you're hanging out with Annie?' Jon yelled at me. "I hit him yesterday, and it was like hitting a wall. It wasn't natural Annie. Who is he? What is he?"

"Thanks for asking how I'm feeling. You shouldn't have hit him," I answered wearily. "Zell didn't do anything to you. He was just protecting me."

"Since when do you need protection?"

"I don't. Zell just seems to think I do."

"Zell, Zell, Zell," Jonny mocked. "I'm getting sick of hearing his name. What kind of name is Zell anyway?"

"An old family name," I retorted beginning to get angry at him.

"Where is his family, Annie? No one has seen any of his family."

"I have seen his father. He is here with him. Zell and his father have a home on Lake Lanier," I said reversing the roles and defending Zell for a change. Zell did say his housekeeper and assistant pose as his parents. Didn't he?

"Oh, so big, bad Zell has already taken you to meet the parents?" Jon asked not believing me.

"Drop dead," I replied coldly pushing past Jon. I stomped off in a huff across the parking lot.

"You'll be sorry you ever met him when I'm finished," Jon yelled after me.

My blood chilled when Jon said those words. I stopped and turned to look at him. His face was dark and brooding. His voice . . . His voice was different. He sounded so malevolent. His voice reminded me of another voice, but I couldn't place where I had heard it. Was it a voice from my nightmares, or had I actually heard it somewhere? I couldn't be sure, but I was shaking from the sound of it.

Zell wasn't in homeroom. Everyone was asking me where he was. I wondered where he was too. I was worried. Maybe he had given up on me and returned to wherever he came from. Where did he come from? I knew the Europe story he told everyone at school, but was that true? I didn't even know for sure.

What if Zell had gone? What would I do the next time a Dark One attacked without him? I didn't dare leave the company of friends without Zell here. I would not be cutting across back lots or staying late for ball practice anymore. Had Zell said something about the Dark Ones would not attack if there were other humans around? I searched my memory, but I could not be sure if he made that statement or if I dreamed that he did. The agonizing day drug by. It was then that I realized he had completely changed my world.

The realization left me empty. Zell had gone. I was sure of it. He had left me, the silly high school senior, who argued with him at every turn. The girl who was determined to do things her way despite the danger it put them both in. He left her at the mercy of the Dark Ones who hunted her watching and waiting because they knew she would not obey him. Her stubbornness and reckless behavior would soon give them their chance to do their master's bidding.

I walked in English class and dropped my books on my desk. With a thud, I dropped my head on top of my books, and I sat there listening to Mrs. Edge's voice drone on and on about figurative language. I expected Mrs. Edge to order me out of the classroom and to the office for having my head on my desk, so I tried to will myself to lift my head. It was of no use. The light of my short existence had walked out of my life, and I was doomed. A frantic, maniacal laughter threatened to spill out over my lips, as I thought about how drastically my life had changed in the last couple of weeks. I had changed from an independent, light-hearted, foolish girl to a somber, head over heels in love teenager with a mission in a week. What was that thought that still swirled around in my head? Head over heels in love? Was it true? If I were honest, it must be true. I had just admitted to being in love with Zell if only to myself. The thought of never seeing him again broke my heart. I groaned, and Mrs. Edge walked my way.

"Are you ill, Annie?" Mrs. Edge bent over me concerned. She was concerned because this person with her head down on her desk groaning was not the light-hearted, fun loving, high-spirited Annie Hayes everyone knew.

"Yesss." I groaned.

"Why don't you go to the school nurse's office, and see if there is anything she can do for you," Mrs. Edge whispered privately to me.

"No, I can't leave," I groaned again not turning my head to look at Mrs. Edge. Knowing I could not be caught alone in an empty stair well by a Dark One, I thought it best to stay put. Stay with the crowd Zell said. Had he said that? Perhaps, it was just in a dream.

Mrs. Edge thinking it must be one of those girly ailments decided it was best to leave me alone and quietly left me.

Lunch was a nightmare. When Jon saw that Zell was not with me, he hurried to sit at my table. I could not eat. I was too upset. Kate and I sat huddled together speculating on what had happened to Zell. I had two fears. The first fear was that Zell had sickened of my rebellious attitude and left me forever. The second fear was that the Dark Ones had come for him. With Zell out of the way, I was an easy target.

"Where's your new boyfriend, Annie?" Jon asked sitting down across the table from Kate and me.

"I don't have a boyfriend, but if you are referring to Zell, I'm not sure. Maybe he is home sick today."

"Oh really," Jon remarked, "Are you sure you haven't just dumped him already."

"Hardly," I replied icily.

"Well, then, perhaps he has dumped you," Jon said sarcastically.

"Get lost, Jon." I snarled turning my back on him and resuming my conversation with Kate.

However, Jon didn't give up so easily.

"Really, Annie, if you and Zell have split, then I want you back."

I rolled my eyes at Kate not even bothering to turn around or respond to him. Jon reached over and grabbed my hand.

"Please Annie."

Jerking my hand out of Jon's grasp, I faced him.

"Leave me alone. Jon, I'm sorry, but we were never going together. You assumed that I was your girlfriend, and you were the closest thing to a boyfriend that I have ever had. Zell and I have not split. We are still friends just like you and I are still friends, but you and I are not exclusive. Zell is my friend now too, and I don't want to give either of you up."

"Then dump the jerk if you want to be with me. I won't share you," Jon hatefully spit out the words.

"Zell is not a jerk. He has been wonderful to me," my voice broke on the word wonderful. Tears sprang to my eyes. I was angry with myself. I did not want to show any weakness to Jon, and here I was almost in tears.

"Ha, I knew it. There *is* trouble in paradise," Jon taunted seeing the tears in my eyes.

"You have no idea what you are talking about," I spouted back at Jon. I'll see you at basketball practice,

Kate." I smiled at Kate as I rose from the crowded lunch table. Then turning to Jon, I locked eyes with him giving him the coldest stare that I could muster. Kate peered around me and made a face at him too.

Walking past him, the lunch room suddenly seemed stifling. I hurried outside. I needed some fresh air. I needed to breathe. I leaned against the exterior wall and inhaled deep breaths of air. Was Jon right? Had Zell dumped me? Where was he? I closed my eyes and squeezed the tears back in. I would not cry here at school. I had to find out where Zell was. I had to. I had to know. Had Zell given up on me? Was he hurt, dead or dying?

My chest began to heave and hurt at just the thought. I have to go to him. I have to find out. A group of students came out of the cafeteria door laughing and talking. I began to walk behind them toward the school office. I would sign out sick. I was sick, heartsick. Thankfully, Mrs. Woods was at lunch, and I would not have to go through an inquisition. There was only a student aide in the office. I quickly signed out and pulled the keys to my car out of my bag.

"Leaving so soon?" I heard the voice as I was pulling open the door to my Tahoe. I stopped, took a deep breath, and turned facing Jon.

"I'm not feeling well. I'm going home." I was sure the pallor of my face supported my statement.

"I bet you're not going home. I bet you're going to him," Jon snarled.

"If I am, it is none of your business," I snarled back at him.

"I totally disagree," Jon stated coldly reaching around me and slamming my car door shut. Roughly, he grabbed my arms and pulled me to him. He tried to press his lips to mine, and I turned my face so quickly that his lips ended up kissing where my hair covered my ear. The bully in Jon reared its ugly head. He began dragging me toward his truck.

"Stop Jonny, you're hurting me," I gasped. Jon ignored my pleas and continued to drag me across the parking lot.

When Jon turned to look back at me, I became frightened. The same black look clouded his face as it had this morning. I started to fight back planting my feet and leaning my weight to the rear. Unfortunately, the bottoms of my shoes were slick, and they would not stay planted. Jon was pulling me along as I tried to hit him with my free hand. The blows that connected were weak as I was trying to swing at him across my body. My arm closest to him was firmly entrenched in his grip. At his car, he slowed. I got lucky and landed a hard lick to his chin. I could see the fury in his eyes. He slammed his keys on the roof. Jon took his free hand and grabbed me by the throat. My backpack dropped to the ground.

"Not even Zell will want you when I'm finished with you," Jon growled. His hand left my throat, and I gasped for air, choking and gagging. Jon grabbed me by the hair and threw me in the passenger seat of his truck. I landed face first with my upper torso on the seat, and my lower half dangled off the edge of the seat. He twisted the arm he had locked in his grasp and pulled it behind my back. As he did so, he reached for my other arm twisting it behind too. Holding both my wrists in just one of his big hands, he pulled off his belt and wrapped it around my wrists. Then he picked up my feet that were hanging half out of the door and threw them inside slamming the door as he did so.

I was in an awkward position with my face pressed in the crevice where the back and the seat met. I tried to find something solid against which to place my feet hoping I could push myself up. Finally, managing to get my feet against the door, I pushed with my feet and with my head against the back of the seat inching myself upward. I gave a final push with my shoulder turning myself as I did so. I was upright again.

"This is kidnapping Jon," I ground out between clenched teeth.

"Really, who says?" he replied looking at me smiling. "You're my girl. I'll say you went voluntarily. Your word against mine."

"You're going to pay for this," I breathed heavily.

"Really, am I?"

"And I'm not your girl," I added.

"Yes, you are. You'll forget all about Zell, by the time I'm finished with you."

"You are evil," I hissed at him.

"If you only knew how evil, you really would be alarmed," Johnny laughed manically.

I believed him. There are many forms of evil in this world, and I now placed Jon firmly on that side. How could I have not seen this side of him? Quite possibly because I had never crossed him before. Others had; I knew that. I also knew that he unfailingly made them pay for their supposed transgression against him. I had just thought it to be the Alpha Male in him. I thought about it: his need to be always right, to always be first, to be on top. He was a driven person. Now, if he couldn't have me, Zell wouldn't either. Zell had sealed our fates with

Jon the day he stood up to him in the cafeteria. Jon would see to it that we both paid for his humiliation and his slip from idol status with the major population of the school. Of that, I was sure.

Zell, where was he? Was he hurt or dead? Surely, he would come for me if he were OK. I had to think. I had to figure out a way to outsmart Jon. Stall him, a voice inside me seemed to say. Give Zell time to find you.

"Jonny, you're right. You're more my type than Zell." I decided that I had to make him believe that he could still be my boyfriend. "Just please let me go. My dad will be worried, and he has suffered enough in this lifetime." Jon refused to answer or even look at me. I lay my head back against the seat thinking.

"Where are we going?" I asked meekly pretending to be over my anger at him.

"To our family cabin on the lake."

Located in a secluded area of Lake Lanier, I knew Jon's cabin. He took me fishing there a couple of summers ago. It wasn't that far from where Zell's house was located, but the mere isolation of it terrified me more than I wanted to show. Thoughts swirled around my head. My head ached from the temporarily halted blood flow when Jon had his big hands around my neck. I needed to play my cards right. Maybe, I can get away from him. I was trying to calm my frantic thoughts and wildly beating heart and come up with a plan at the same time.

"I'm living in a horror show," I murmured aloud and turned looking out the window.

"Did you say something?" Jon asked.

"Yes, I said my life is a horror show," I yelled at him as though he were deaf.

Jon said nothing. He just looked at me like I had lost my mind.

Jon didn't know the half of it. He didn't know of the monstrous wolf-like creature in the parking lot of the school, the vampire on the beach when he went for my sweater, nor of the monster that lurked near the dumpsters at school. My life had turned into a freak show. Monsters lurked in the shadows waiting for me. I could not live my life normally anymore. I had to think before I did the slightest thing. The wrong move could put my life in jeopardy. Just like deciding to take a shortcut to the gym, I had made that trip dozens of times. This time I took the shortcut, and a monster lay waiting for me. How many other vulnerable moments had other dark beings discovered in my daily life. Evidently, they watched from shadowy hiding places. They waited, and calculated weaknesses in my defenses. At any time, they could exploit those weaknesses. My shoulders, arms, and wrists ached. I could not sit comfortably with my hands tied behind me.

Where was Zell? He was so quiet after the last attack. He saw me safely home and walked out of my life without a word. Realizing he could never protect me because I would not allow him total access to my life, Zell must have walked away not wanting to see the massacre that was coming. My independent nature drove him from me. All he ever wanted was to be at my side to protect me. Then, I would do something stupid like stealing away when he was occupied with Miss Picknell. After that, he, most likely in a panic to find me, comes upon me seconds before I am to be devoured by a hideous monster. I could tell the images of what would have happened to me had he arrived seconds later had upset him. I am sure he didn't want to stick around to witness my death at the hands of the Dark Ones, and he had fled. Pain darted up my arms to my shoulders and roused me from my dark thoughts. I must convince Jon to untie me.

"Jon," I said sweetly.

"What?" he muttered.

"Sitting with my hands tied behind me is really uncomfortable. Would you untie my hands? Please."

Jon turned slightly to look at me and snorted.

"Not a chance," he laughed.

I grunted twisting my face up. Obviously, I'm not much of an actress.

It was beginning to be apparent that Zell was not coming for me. At this point, he would not have a clue where to look. Even if he had not disappeared as quickly and as suddenly as he came into my life, he would never look for me with Jon. Hope was beginning to slip away. I closed my eyes and leaned back against the seat.

Determined, I opened my eyes again. If Zell was not coming for me, I had to get away from Jon myself. I would have to be ready when the chance came. I have to try and get my hands free. Escape would be difficult with both of my hands tied behind my back.

Jon turned off the highway on to a gravel road. He turned to me and grabbed me roughly. He yanked my chin up and kissed me. If I had doubts before that Jon was not the one for me, that kiss sealed it. I felt nothing.

"You'll thaw out when we get to the cabin." Jon released me and put the truck back in gear.

Was that a threat? I wondered.

Forests thickly lined the sides of the road. Large, muddy pits accented the gravel drive. My heart sank deeper and deeper into an abyss of despair the further we drove into the woods and away from the main road. It would be impossible for someone to locate me here. Furthermore, it would be a nightmare trying to escape. On foot, it would take me hours to get back to the main road. If I managed to escape, I decided that I would follow the road but stay hidden in the woods.

The deep ruts in the road made the truck lurch back and forth throwing me around the cab of the truck violently. I could not break the tossing and falling with my hands as they were tied securely behind me. I was sure to be black and blue with bruises. Then, the truck hit a particularly deep rut. I lurched forward, and a sharp pain reverberated through my head. Blackness clouded my vision. Then nothingness.

10.   KIDNAPPED

I AWOKE TO MOVEMENT. JON WAS carrying me toward a rickety-looking cabin sitting about fifty feet from the lake. The shore was mostly a tangled mess of vines and weeds. This looked to be more of hunting and fishing cabin than a vacation cabin. I peeked out from under my eyelashes surveying the landscape. I did not want Jon to know that I was conscious again. He must have untied me because my arms were dangling loosely at my sides. It was probably too awkward for him to carry me with my hands tied behind my back.

Jon was definitely a muscle-man. He carried me effortlessly. My face was nestled against a bulging bicep. I exerted extreme effort to remain motionless. Conceivably, if Jon thought I was unconscious, he would not tie my hands again. Perhaps, he would lay me down and leave me alone for a while waiting on me to gain consciousness. I did my best to peruse the environment around the cabin for possible escape routes. Trying to look without moving my head, I thought I caught a glimpse of a boat dock in the distance. Cautiously, I opened my eyes a little wider. There was a small fishing boat with a motor tied to the dock. I worried that it may not have gas or be hard to start. If I were to get away, I would have to be able to start it the first time. Jon would be alerted by the noise of the failed start of the boat. It was what was tied to the other side of the dock that lifted my spirits. There on the opposite side of the dock from the boat was a canoe almost as large as the fishing boat. If I could get away, I could use it to escape quietly.

Jon suddenly shifted me in his arms. As focused as I was on the canoe, I almost yelped in surprise— almost. He was just reaching for a hidden key behind a light on the porch. Precariously, he balanced me on his knee while he freed one hand to unlock the cabin door. I heard the lock click, and Jon pushed open the door. The door creakingly protested, and he gave it another shove. Pocketing the key, he slid his arm under me again. As he strode into the room, a damp musty smell invaded my senses. There was also a faint smell of fish that was most likely a remnant of the last visit here. Jon crossed the room and kicked open a door.

He walked in a few steps and dumped me on a foul-smelling mattress. Still, I feigned unconsciousness. I could feel rather than see Jon lean over me. I must look like a ghost because he pressed two fingers to my neck to see if I had a pulse. Satisfied that I was not dead, I could hear him move away from the bed. Straining to listen, I heard the latch on the door click. Cautiously, I peered out from under my lashes, in case he was still in the room. Satisfied the room was empty, I opened my eyes wide to look around. The dark room was bare except for the bed upon which I lay and a small bedside table with a sad, dusty lamp. Even though it was mid-afternoon, the room was dimly lit. The walls were planks of musty, dark wood instead of drywall. The small window did not receive direct sunlight at this time of day.

Carefully, I tested the mattress to see if it squeaked. The squeaks were mainly in the center of the bed, so I cautiously edged to the perimeter of the mattress. A banging from the other room ceased my progress.

"There is no food in this whole damn house," I heard Jon swearing as he banged the cupboard doors open and shut. I used the noise to cover my escape from the bed. I moved toward the single window to see if it would open. I tried the latch, and it slid to the unlocked position which surprised me considering its rusty state. With doors still banging open and shut, I tried the window. It resisted. I tried again putting more effort into opening the window. It began to rise. The racket in the next room ceased, and I froze. I heard Jon's footsteps coming closer to the room. I slid the window back down and headed for the bed.

Easing on to the bed, I feigned unconsciousness again as Jon burst through the door. Jon quickly crossed the room. Grabbing my wrist, he tied a piece of frazzled rope to it. I involuntarily groaned as he grabbed my other wrist tying it to the first. I was already sore from the tortuous ride in the truck and having my hands tied behind my back which had strained muscles in my arms, neck, and back. At least, he was tying my hands in front this time. I tried to make space between my two wrists without Jon noticing. He took the other end of the rope and tied it to the bedpost. Then he huffed off slamming the door as he went. I heard the front door close moments later. Straining to listen for the truck, I breathed a sigh of relief when I heard gravels crunching outside as his truck drove down the drive.

Twisting my wrists back and forth, I tried to free my hands. I managed a little wiggle room in my efforts but not enough to free them. Jon had not tied my hands behind me, and he had not tied my right hand to the bedpost just the other end of the rope. That meant I should be able to untie the rope. I sat up and scooted toward the bedpost. It definitely wasn't easy, but I managed to work one knot loose. I tugged and pulled at the other knot. I know Jon must have been in a hurry, or he would have been much more careful about leaving me securely tied up. I figured he wanted to get to wherever he was headed and back before dark. What time was it? I had no idea, but I guessed I had a couple of hours of daylight left. What if a dark creature tracked me here? The thought of facing one alone sent shivers down my spine, and I speeded up my efforts to get free.

My arms ached and my wrists burned like fire from being tied up, but I still persisted. Finally, my efforts were rewarded, and the last knot slipped loose. My hands were still tied, but I was free from the prison of the bed. Cautiously, I went to the bedroom door and listened. It was possible that during my intense concentration while untying the rope that Jon had returned. I listened for any sounds coming from the next room for a long minute. When I was satisfied that he was not there, I quietly turned the knob and cracked the door open. Still no sign of him. I slid through the door and closed it behind me. I did not want him to notice an open door when he returned. Perhaps he would have to go to the bathroom, or he may fix himself something to eat before he checks on me. Minutes were precious in this situation. Minutes could be the difference between freedom and whatever Jon had planned for me. I still didn't want to think about what Jon could be capable of. If he thought I was still tied up in the bedroom, it could buy me precious minutes on the run.

I crossed the room to the kitchen silently. A knife lying on the kitchen counter next to a roll of black duct tape chilled my blood. Why had Jon had a knife out? On closer inspection, I noticed rope fibers sticking to the end of the knife. Perhaps, his only intention for the knife was to cut the rope. I desperately wished it to be so. Jon and I had been friends for years. I could not believe he wished me harm. Even though he had kidnapped me, I realized it was an act of desperation and jealously. He was insanely jealous of Zell of that I was sure. I thought of Zell and paused. I missed him so much, and it had only been less than twenty-four hours since I last saw him. It seemed like forever though. How had Zell existed for an eternity without a family or someone to love? I pitied him then. I was sorry for every mean thing I had ever said to him. I wanted to see him now more than anything I had ever wanted in my life. I missed him desperately. Where was he?

"Snap out of this," I reprimanded myself out loud. "First things first. You have to get yourself out of these ropes." I grabbed the hilt of the knife. Awkwardly, I attempted to saw at the rope where it crossed over my hand.

"Oh," I said sickly as the knife sliced through my flesh. It was difficult to control the blade with my wrists still tied. However, I could see I was making progress. Several strands of the rope lay severed. I twisted and turned my wrists and another strand that had been cut halfway through popped open. My efforts sent streams of blood running down my hands and pooling on the counter. I continued to saw away at the rope intermittently cutting my hand as I did so. Finally, enough of the rope had been cut to enable me to slip my bloody hand free. I dropped the knife, and it clattered to the counter. The sound unnerved me, and I looked furtively around expecting someone to jump on me. I pulled the rope from my hands. I opened the door beneath the sink and threw the rope remnants in the dark back corner. I then washed the knife and laid it back on the counter. I opened drawers looking for a kitchen towel or something to clean up the bloody mess on the counter. I finally found what I was looking for. Two badly stained but clean kitchen towels were stuffed in a drawer with some fishing lures. I took out the most stained one and wet it under the faucet. I wiped down the bloody counter. I was still dripping blood everywhere. I took the second towel and wrapped it around my hand. Tearing off a long strip of duct tape, I wound it around the towel holding it in place. I finished cleaning up my blood from the counter and floor, and then I threw the towel under the sink in the same dark corner where I had thrown the rope.

"Now, what do I do?" I sank to the kitchen floor deep in thought. Something vibrated against my leg. I blinked. My cell phone! My cell phone was in my pocket. I thought I had put it in my book bag in English class. I knew my book bag was lying in the parking lot next to where Jon's truck had been.

Eagerly, I dug in my pocket with my good hand and pulled out my phone.

"Oh, thank God," I said with a heartfelt sigh.

I looked at the number. It was Zell.

"Help me, Zell," I whispered into the phone.

"Annie, where are you?" Zell's voice sounded frantic.

"Jon kidnapped me. I think he brought me to a family fishing cabin on Lake Lanier." I whispered into the phone. I knew Jon was not there, but I still could not make myself talk in a normal voice. "Where have you been?"

"I went to my shop to make some special weapons. I wanted you to have something with which to defend yourself since you seem to be determined to wander around alone. I thought you would be safe at school. After yesterday, I thought you would stick close by your friends at least for a few days. I came to meet you after school. I found your book bag in the parking lot, and your car was still parked in the lot. Kate and I have been calling and searching for you for over two hours." I could hear a trace of panic in his voice.

"I must not have had service because this is the first time the phone has rung. I didn't even know I had it on me until just now. I've got to go. Jon left for a few minutes. I think I am miles from the main road. There is a boat and a canoe by the dock. If I am on the lake, can you search for me by air?" I asked Zell still whispering as if someone were close by.

"Yes, I will find you," Zell whispered back as if someone were listening to him also.

"Zell?" I called to him.

"Yes, sweetheart," he answered.

[201]

My heart melted at his term of endearment.

"I . . . I . . . I'm sorry. I'm sorry about everything. I believe you. I believe you are who you say you are. I believe you are from the race of the Anak. I believe that your father is a Fallen Angel, a Watcher. I do believe my life is in danger, and you are here to protect me. I'm glad that you are here. I can't even remember what my life was like before you. You are my life now too," I murmured so lightly that I wasn't even sure he heard me.

"I just wanted you to know in case . . . in case this ends badly."

"It won't. I am coming for you Annie."

I ended my call and closed my eyes. I was just thankful that Zell had not left, and that I had heard his voice once more before . . . . I had a premonition that this would not end well. I could not shake the feeling. I sat in the floor with my phone clutched to my chest and my eyes closed for several minutes before I could shake myself out of the melancholy that I felt.

"Get up," I said aloud. "Get up now!" I pushed myself up from the kitchen floor willing my bruised and exhausted body to move. I went to the front door, but it had a dead bolt. It was the kind of dead bolt that needed a key to get out. I searched the rest of the cabin for a key or a back door. There was a back door in the kitchen, but it also had a dead bolt and needed a key to unlock it. I searched the sparse rooms, but I could not find a key. Jon must have the only key. I hurried back to the bedroom shutting the door. I crossed to the window and pushed it up. I put first one leg and then another over the window sill. Next, I turned so the sill was under my belly. I pushed myself out of the window. It was a seven or eight-foot drop to the ground, but I landed easily.

I ran in a panic to the dock. I hoped a key would be in the boat, but I doubted it. Double-checking, I looked in the boat for a key. There was no key. I crossed to the motor and pulled the hose that went from the gas tank to the motor out. I threw it as far into the lake as I could manage. It did not sink but floated on top of the water. I just hoped it sank before Jon got back. If Jonny had a key and got the boat started, he could overtake me in no time rowing a canoe. Climbing back on to the dock, I crossed to the other side and jumped in the canoe. My hopes lifted when I saw two oars strapped to each side of the canoe.

Hurriedly, I untied the canoe from the moorings and pushed the canoe away from the docks. Dropping on the tiny bench between the oars, I grabbed an oar in each hand. I had never rowed before. It took several minutes of experimenting before I could head out into open water. The effort broke open the wounds on my hand. Blood soaked the towel. I ignored the blood and the pain and rowed. I rowed as if my life depended on it. Perhaps, it did. Lake Lanier was northeast of school. If I wanted to head back in the direction we came from, wouldn't I need to row southwest? The sun would be setting in the west, and I headed in the direction just to the left of the setting sun. I rowed and rowed until the muscles in my back and arms seemed to be in knots, yet I didn't see a house or dock anywhere. I rested letting the canoe drift with the current.

While I rested, my thoughts went wild. Who would find me first: Jon, Zell, or a Dark One? I searched the sky for Zell, but it was empty except for a few billowy clouds. I thought I heard a boat motor in the distance. I panicked. Could it possibly be Jon? I looked along the shore looking for a place to land and hide the canoe until the boat went past, or I was sure it wasn't him. I had mixed feelings about hiding the boat. How would Zell find me if I were hiding? I heard the sound of a motor again, and it was getting louder. I decided that I would hide until the boat passed, then I would get back out on the lake. I began rowing furiously for the shore. Hopefully, the bend would hide me until I drug the canoe out and into the trees. About fifteen feet from shore, I jumped from the boat. Holding the rope that tied the canoe to the dock, I drug it. If I had thought rowing was hard, dragging this canoe was almost impossible. I managed to get it to land. I went to the bow and lifted it up. Then backing up, I pulled the canoe into the shelter of trees and a few bushes. I hid behind the canoe and waited for the boat to come around the bend.

I huddled behind the canoe in the trees hoping it would not be noticed. As the boat came around the corner, my heart sank. It was Jon. He was looking along the shore. He slowed the motor of the boat. I began edging toward the thick woods. He must have noticed the canoe because his motor died. It was then that I saw the tracks the canoe had left as I pulled it from the water to the trees. The tracks alerted Jon. I jumped up in a dead run. It was getting dark. Perhaps, he would be unable to find me in the dark.

Panic stricken, I ran. It was just like my nightmare. I could hear something thrashing about in the woods behind me. I tripped over a large root that protruded from the earth. Landing in the soft decaying leaves, I breathed heavily. I was drenched from head to toe from jumping out of the boat. Leaves and dirt clung to my wet skin and clothing. This day had just about done me in. I was aching all over. My hand throbbed under the blood-soaked towel that was still wrapped around it. I just wanted to lay here and rest. I was exhausted from rowing in the canoe.

I had to keep going. Wearily, I pushed myself up. I was halfway on my feet when I was tackled from behind. I landed on my stomach again with someone or something on top of me. I spat out dirt and decayed leaves from my mouth. Twisting, I turned to see who was on top of me. Of course, it was Jon.

"Get off of me," I screamed at him.

"Not until I'm through with you," he growled. Jon tried to kiss me, but I crossed my arms in front of my face trying to push him off. That is when I heard it. Something big was coming through the woods growling as it came.

"Stop. Jon listen. We're not alone in the woods. Something is coming."

Jon continued trying to pull my hands from my face, but he must have heard it, too. He stopped struggling with me and lay still listening. It sounded as though a bulldozer was coming through the woods. I could hear not just twigs but small trees snapping as something came in our direction.

"What the . . ." Jon began.

"Shhhhh," I whispered as I clamped my good hand over his mouth.

In the filtered moonlight, I could see large red eyes moving in our direction. The eyes looked to be about ten feet off the ground. Whatever it is, it is enormous. When it was fifty feet from us, I could make out another feature. White, gigantic fangs gleamed in the faint moonlight. Jon must have seen them too. He jumped to his feet, and without another word to me, he ran into the night.

"Coward," I hissed in the direction which he ran. I scrambled to my feet. I backed up trying to keep this newest monster in my line of vision. Maybe if I could get back to Jon's fishing boat, I would have a chance at escape. Besides, Zell would be looking for me on the lake. I had to get to him. I began to run through the forest back in the direction I had just come. Stumbling over roots and small trees, I ran. I could hear the thing behind me pick up the pace. I ran flying through the trees which I could faintly see in the moonlight, but it wasn't good enough. I could hear the creature gaining on me. The dark trees became sparser, and I broke into an open area. I turned my head to see how close the beast was behind me. Only a few feet separated us. Then it leaped. The impact hit me like a train. I could feel teeth sinking into my body. The pain hit instantly. It radiated out from where the creature sank in its teeth and burned like I was on fire. I thought of Zell. I thought of my father. Would they miss me? Of course they would, I scolded myself. Another strong impact, I felt my flesh tearing. Was it eating me now?

"Is this what death feels like?" I wondered. It felt more like I was floating on a cloud than in the jaws of a monster. The pain was horrific but quick. There was no pain now.

"Annie, are you OK?" I thought I heard Zell's voice. This isn't so bad I thought. There is no pain, and I can still remember Zell's voice.

Then I felt his warm lips pressed to my forehead, and his strong arms were around me.

"Am I dead?" I asked.

"No. No, you are not dead. You are very much alive," he whispered.

"Where is the monster?"

"Still in the woods," Zell replied.

"Where am I?" I whispered softly.

"You are with me," he answered pressing his face to mine. I could feel rather than see tears escape his eyes and fall against my face.

"You found me," I said simply.

"Yes, I found you," he whispered holding me close.

Only then did I open my eyes. No longer was the moon faintly peeking through the trees. It was big, bright, and large. It looked so close. It was with that thought that I realized we were airborne. I felt safe. Zell's arms were around me, and I could hear his heart beating against my cheek as he held me to him. If I died now, death was acceptable. Zell had come for me and found me. I was at peace.

Zell had spotted Jon on the lake and followed him to me. He had swooped down, and the impact and tearing of flesh that I had felt had actually been Zell diving from the sky to steal me from the monster's jaws and ripping me free from its deadly grip.

"I have to get you to a hospital. That thing bit you," Zell whispered against the wind of the night his voice breaking.

"Bit me?" Then blackness consumed me again for the second time today.

11. ZELL

THE HOLLOWNESS OF THAT MOMENT
confounded him. He dreamed of her for too long.
When Annie was born, belonging was birthed in him.
He knew that with her was where he belonged no
matter where that journey took him. He always
dreamed that if he ever revealed himself to her that
she would know she belonged to him, too. That's not
exactly how it played out. She did not like him at all.
She fought his every move to protect her. Though
lately, he could tell her feelings were changing.

He had always wanted heaven. He grew up
striving for that place. When he touched Annie for the
first time that night in the parking lot at school, he
found his eternal world in her. In all his wanderings
through this world of grief, he finally found her—the
other half of his heart. All of everything came into
existence in Annie. She could not die on him. A dry
sob escaped from Zell's lips as he held Annie as close
as he possibly could.

Annie's eyes fluttered open for a brief moment and focused on him. She smiled warmly at him.

"Zell, I . . . ," Annie began weakly and ceased to breathe.

Don't miss the sequel and second novel, *Forever Girl*, in the Anak Trilogy.

Preview

Forever Girl

1. GUILT

JON RAN FOR ONLY A FEW YARDS WHEN HE suddenly stopped. Annie, how could he leave her there with that . . . that thing? Undecided, he stood there. He loved Annie. Ever since that new guy Zell had come to school, she had not given him the time of day. He wanted to make her pay for ignoring him. He wanted to make her pay for dropping him and giving Zell all her attention. He wanted to make them both pay for the humiliation that he felt in the cafeteria. He had made it clear to the guys at school that Annie was exclusively his. He had thoroughly terrorized them, so no guy dared to speak to Annie for more than a few minutes.

Then, Zell showed up, and he couldn't be intimidated. Every time he had confronted Zell, Zell had stood up to him. He silently dared Jon to continue. Jon knew Zell would pursue Annie if he wanted, and there was nothing he could do about it. If he stepped over the line with Zell, he knew there would be a fight. Jon enjoyed a rumble now and then, but not one he couldn't win. He didn't think he would win a fight with Zell; though, he had nothing to give him that feeling but instinct. Something about that guy was different. He exuded an aura of perpetual danger.

He loved Annie, yet he had left her there for a monster to tear to shreds. Would Zell have left her? Somehow he didn't think so, and the thought shamed him.

What was that thing? It had been several feet taller than him who at six feet, three inches and two hundred and twenty pounds of muscle was a tenacious force himself. Fingers of panic and remorse grabbed at his chest. He couldn't leave Annie. He started back toward the sound of Annie's scream. He had just made it back to her when he saw the creature had her in its grasp. He had thought the creature might have been a large bear, but this thing that had Annie was no bear. It was a hairy mountain with long, sharp teeth. This was a monster from the pit of hell. One thing Jon was sure of, this was not a natural creature but a supernatural one.

As he stood by helpless, trying to figure out how to distract the monster. Another creature swooped from the sky and scooped Annie right from the mouth of the beast. The creature tried to clamp its jaws down on Annie to prevent her escape, but its enormous fangs just ripped through the flesh of her legs as if they were butter when the being tore her from its jaws. The great beast stood on its hind legs and screamed into the night. Jon covered his ears. The sound terrified him.

What beast was this that had Annie now? Jon knew it had wings, but it had dropped from the sky so swiftly and snatched her so quickly that it took him and the creature by surprise. Jon disappeared behind a tree and leaned against it. Where was Annie? The thing that snatched her had great wings and was amazingly huge, but it was some form of a man—of that he was sure. Had the creature saved her or was she in even more danger? For all he knew, the second creature may have already killed Annie. What was it people said when something like that happened? Out of the frying pan and into the fire? The monster was still roaring and screaming. Jon was trembling. He climbed into the midst of some plant overgrowth that was growing between several trees. He curled into a ball and waited there for the monster to stop screeching and leave.

Jon was filled with remorse. This was all his fault. Annie's blood was on his hands. He brought her here. He was sure she was dead, and he had made her last hours alive horrific. He had kidnapped her, thrown her in his truck, and brought her to the cabin in the woods. She had escaped and run from him when he had driven to the nearest store for supplies. He had kidnapped her in a jealous rage, and he had not planned this well at all. When he got to the cabin, there was nothing to eat or drink. He didn't plan on letting her go anytime soon, and that made a trip to the store a necessity. He was going to keep her until he was ready to let her go, and that wouldn't be until she was in love with him. He was going to make her love him. She would be his and his alone before he would take her back. She would forget all about Zell. Zell would not want her anyway after he finished telling him all the intimate details about their nights alone in the cabin. Zell would hate her, and that is what he wanted.

Annie was gorgeous. The most beautiful thing about her was that she didn't realize how beautiful she was. Her blond hair fell to her waist, and her big, blue eyes were always smiling. She had a peaceful spirit about her that was the opposite of his tumultuous one. She was slim but perfectly built, and Jon had decided in seventh grade that he had to have her. Then, *he* came. Jon was so consumed with jealously that he never considered what would happen to him if somehow Annie freed herself and went to the police. Blindly, he believed that if she were alone with him, she would forget all about Zell. Now, she was gone, and he would never see her again. Jon put his head in his hands and began to weep silently. It was then that he heard the snapping of twigs and branches all around him. He shook violently. Was the creature still there? Were there more of them? Was it looking for him? Jon held his breath and waited. He could barely control the violent shaking that overtook him. He had to control it, or the monster would find him. The monster roared and screamed again only feet from the brush where Jon was hiding.

A retired school teacher, Sherry Fortner, now writes romance and paranormal novels fulltime from her home in Southeastern Tennessee where she lives with her husband, Ray, her horses, Misty, Gummy Bear, and Spice, two Yorkshire terriers, Elvis and Belle, barn cats, Boo-Boo Kitty and Cloud, and assorted chickens. Dark Angel is her debut release in the Anak Trilogy. When not writing, Sherry can be found outside in her garden, riding around her ranch, or playing with her grandchildren or animals. Visit Sherry at her website at www.sherryfortner.com .

Made in the USA
Charleston, SC
09 July 2015